Welcome To Nightmare Island

Devin Cabrera

Copyright © 2023 Devin Cabrera
All rights reserved.
ISBN 9798386803124
Cover art by Greg Chapman

Chapter One

Jonah awoke with a start. Through half-closed eyelids he looked at the clock on his bedside table: 3 AM. He groaned and shifted in his blankets. Blinking rapidly, Jonah struggled to get his eyes to adjust to the darkness.

Shadows of tree branches danced across the walls of his room as light from the moon cast its glow through the open window. He watched as the curtains billowed along with the cold breeze that floated in.

Something didn't feel right about the room. Did he leave the window open? Of course not, it was the middle of winter. The hairs on the back of his neck pricked up. It felt like someone was watching him. Jonah cast his gaze around the room, searching for the culprit.

That's when he saw it. A massive dark shadow was lurking at the foot of his bed. Jonah tried to look closer, to make out what it was, but his eyes were still adjusting to the lack of light in the room.

Then the shadow began to move, inching closer to Jonah. He sat bolt upright in his bed, eyes glued to the moving shadow coming ever closer. Suddenly, a pair of thick gnarled hands reached out of the darkness, visible only through the moonlight coming in through the window. He screamed as the hands curled around his ankles and pulled.

Then he woke up.

Audrey was shaking Jonah's foot. "Wake up babe, we're gonna be late," she said. Satisfied that his eyes were finally open, she walked out of the room to wake up one of their other sleeping friends.

Jonah looked around the room, searching for the dark shadows, the unknown creature with those thick gnarled hands.

He didn't see anything.

Taking in some ragged breaths, he reached onto the nightstand for his inhaler. Finding it, he brought it to his face and took two steady pulls from the container. He steadied himself, allowing a few moments for his breathing to return to normal. Rolling over, he grabbed his notebook from his bedside table and jotted down a few notes about his dream. Jonah allowed himself to relax a little before switching his gaze over to the alarm clock again. 7 AM.

Shit, they really were going to be late, Jonah thought.

He threw off his blanket, rushing over to the dresser to get changed.

"Does everyone have everything they need?" Audrey called out from the other room. A chorus of yes's could be heard throughout the house. "Then let's go, I'd be a much happier person if we didn't get stuck in traffic on the way there."

Their group of friends were about to leave for the next stop on their yearly horror trip. They were horror junkies, and every October since college they had taken a trip to spooky places throughout the country. Other people liked horror movie marathons, they preferred the real thing.

In the past they had gone to Salem, Massachusetts -- the location of the witch trials, the Amityville Horror house, the Charles Manson house, and many more. This year they had something new in mind. A brand-new horror-filled attraction that was supposed to be scarier than all the rest combined. Needless to say, they were thrilled.

Welcome To Nightmare Island

Jonah grabbed a brass pocket watch from the top of his nightstand. Fitting in the palm of his hand, the pocket watch shell was ornately decorated like nothing he had ever seen. The casing had a carved insignia of a ram skull over a pentagram.

The brass front had been rubbed down, worn by countless hands passing over it.

It had been a gift from Jonah's father and had been passed down from his father before him, and his father before him as well. For countless generations, this watch had been in the family. And now it belonged to Jonah.

He stopped, opening the watch to reveal a photo of his parents under its lid. They had both died tragically in a car accident when he was younger, leaving him to be raised by his grandfather.

His grandfather had been a little crazy. A very eccentric old man who seemed a tad obsessed with the existence of ghosts, which he passed down to his grandson Jonah.

He slipped the watch into his pocket and left the room.

Jonah's friends began filing through the hallway, each dragging their luggage behind them.

First came Annie and Chuck. These two had met in college and had been joined at the hip ever since. Annie was originally a friend of Audrey's, and Chuck was a friend of Jonah's. One day they each decided to bring a friend as a plus one and they hit it off immediately. Chuck was tall, handsome, and voted "most likely to succeed" in high school. Chuck's father was one of the most successful lawyers in their area, and he instilled that drive to succeed in his son as well. He received perfect grades in school and was even captain of the school football team. Chuck followed in his father's footsteps of protecting the innocent, and soon after college, he became a deputy at the local sheriff's office, where his large frame tended to come in handy.

Annie wasn't that bad looking herself. She was blonde with blue eyes, and legs that went on for days. Athletic in her own right, she led her college tennis team to its first championship in half a century. Annie came to a stop beside them with her pink luggage by her side.

Devin Cabrera

Jonah heard a commotion coming from the hallway and knew that Kevin was close behind. Kevin was the third wheel of their group. While the rest of the group was out doing couple things, Kevin tended to make fun of them for public displays of affection, that is, unless he was trying to track down a date of his own at whatever fine establishment that they were at. Kevin was short and hot-tempered, and easily the funniest person in the group. What he lacked in height, he made up for in charisma.

Right now, Kevin was dragging a suitcase bigger than he was. Using two hands to pull his luggage down the hall, he managed to bump and scrape every surface in the house on the way to the door. Huffing and puffing, he looked around at the rest of the group in the living room and said, "Y'all see I'm struggling here, and yet none of you decided to come and help me. I hope I break something on the way out and y'all end up having to pay for it."

Smirking, Chuck said, "What did you pack that's so heavy? It's only a three-day trip."

Whipping his head around to address Chuck directly, Kevin said, "I'm still a bachelor, which means I have to worry about my looks. I gotta bring my weights, my skin products, my hair products, my protein, my creatin. Y'all have dates, you don't have to worry about impressing the ladies anymore. And it's obvious that y'all have stopped trying long ago." Kevin took a second to appraise Jonah and Chuck's outfits with disgust.

"What's wrong with what I'm wearing?" Jonah asked, looking down at his own ensemble.

"The question is, what is right with what you're wearing? And the answer is nothing. You look ridiculous," Kevin said, grinning.

"Oh hush, you two," Audrey said rushing into the room. "You both look fine. Hurry up and get into the car." She stopped by Jonah's side to give him a morning kiss.

Audrey was tall and good looking, but her looks were usually hidden behind a book. Most days you could barely see her brunette locks peeking out from a good horror book. Reading was her biggest hobby, with a room at their house devoted solely to books for her to dive into and get lost in a story that wasn't her own.

That was probably one of the biggest things that attracted her to Jonah. He was an author, and Audrey was his biggest fan. He had written several well-known horror books including: *The Coven in Connecticut, Death Row,* and everyone's favorite *The Woman in Room 666*. Countless days when dealing with writer's block he would sit at the table across from her and they would work through whatever dilemma he was facing. Audrey would be talking animatedly, getting involved in the story and the characters like only a true fan would. Her suggestions had made it into several of his published novels, and they adorn her bookshelf with pride.

It all started about a month ago. Audrey was working away at the stove making breakfast. Jonah was sitting at the kitchen table, flipping through the pages of a newspaper. Suddenly two shadows appeared beneath the front door. Someone was standing outside.

They probably wouldn't have noticed if it weren't for the letter. They heard a scrape on the floor and they each turned to see that a black envelope had been slid under the door.

They stopped what they were doing, Jonah stooping to pick up the letter as Audrey looked on, wiping her hands on a dish towel.

The envelope was addressed to them but didn't have a return sender. They found it strange that the envelope had been delivered to them this way. Usually, any mail they received would be forwarded to their PO box.

Jonah opened the door, expecting to see the person who had delivered the letter. But nobody was there. In fact, after a brief scan, there appeared to be no sign of life on the street. Biting his lip, Jonah closed the door.

He flipped the envelope over. It had been sealed with red wax, and a crest had been stamped into it. Grabbing a letter opener, he pried into it, opening the envelope to reveal a matching black invitation. In metallic gold lettering, it read:

Devin Cabrera

Nightmare Island welcomes Jonah Peterson and party to its grand opening! Nightmare Island is the newest and most up-to-date horror attraction, now featuring real ghosts!

Jonah turned the invitation over, expecting to see additional info on the backside, but there was none to be had. Being a published horror author, there was no shortage of invitations to haunted attractions. Most invites promised to have the most haunted house in the world, or have ghost sightings on the regular, with a quick Google search of reviews proving most to be a hoax. Many of the owners of such places just wanted Jonah to show up so they could get a few pictures of a famous horror writer at their location. Jonah, however, wasn't really interested in boosting the credibility of every mom-and-pop horror shop that sprung up recently. He wasn't interested in appealing to those trying to make a buck off his presence.

However, something about this seemed different. He didn't know if it was the amount of effort they put into the invitation, or the way they managed to track down the location of his vacation home that made him decide to accept the invitation and go to the attraction.

Hell, he thought to himself, I could use the extra inspiration for my new book. He already had the publishers breathing down his neck for some new pages. What's the worst that could happen?

Chapter Two

"Are we almost there yet?" Kevin asked for probably the fiftieth time that day. They had been traveling for six hours on their way to the haunted attraction. If there was ever one person who you did not want to travel with, it would surely be Kevin. He had the bladder of either an infant or an eighty-year-old man. Because of him, the trip must have lasted at least a full hour longer than it was supposed to. Every hour on the hour, Kevin had to pee.

It was an endless cycle of stopping at a gas station to let Kevin pee. Once he was done, he would claim that he was thirsty, and he would pick up a drink while they were stopped. When they were back on the road again, Kevin would down the whole bottle and immediately have to pee again. Repeat the process over and over again.

Right now, Kevin was sitting in the backseat between Chuck and Annie. Normally the couple would sit together, but Kevin was the only one small enough to fit in the middle seat, a fact that pissed him off to no end.

Jonah got the idea that Kevin was asking to stop more to stretch his cramped body out rather than actually having to use the bathroom.

"Are we there yet?" Kevin repeated.

"For the last time, no, we aren't there yet. It's only been five minutes since you asked the last time," Jonah said.

"Well, we better be there soon, I have to pee again," Kevin complained. He shifted in his seat trying to get comfortable, and in the process, he pushed against Chuck and Annie's shoulders, pressing each of them into their respective doors. Jonah's Honda Civic obviously wasn't meant to fit three grown adults in the backseat, especially not when one of them was Chuck's size.

"Well, unless you want to go behind a tree, you're out of luck for a while," Jonah said.

Their navigation system had recently had them pull off the main road that they had been traveling on. Instead insisting that the fastest route to their destination would be down a long dark dirt road going through the middle of a forest.

"What? Do you really expect me to do my business in the woods?" Kevin said. "What if I get poison ivy on my junk? What if I'm standing there urinating and a bear comes up to me mid-pee? I can't just cut it off mid-stream Jonah, I'm not built that way. There must be a gas station or fast-food place around here somewhere."

A quick glance around proved to show no sign of life within visible range. Nothing could be seen past the thick foliage and tree cover.

Jonah swerved to avoid a fallen limb on the road and ended up hitting a large pothole, to the chagrin of his passengers.

"That's it!" Kevin said holding his bladder. "If you keep driving like that, I'm gonna end up pissing all over your car."

At this, Chuck smirked while looking out of his window.

Kevin squirmed out from between Chuck and Annie. He reached his way to the center console. "I'm sure I can find a place to stop somewhere on this map." With that, Kevin began pinching and poking the touchscreen of the navigation system. But it wasn't his car,

Welcome To Nightmare Island

and Kevin had no idea what he was doing. In the process, he ended up throwing the whole navigation system out of whack.

"Great, now we don't know where we're going" Jonah protested.

Audrey reached into the glovebox, found the invitation with the address, and retyped it into the navigation system. The system accepted the address, then a rerouting sign appeared on the screen. A pinwheel on the screen began to spin in circles as the navigation system struggled to load the map again.

Chuck took out his phone. "It's not going to work, there's no service whatsoever in these woods."

The group all turned to glare at Kevin.

"This wouldn't have happened if you had found a place for me to use the bathroom like I asked," Kevin said.

Jonah was about to say something to retort, but then Annie pointed toward the windshield. "Look, there's something out there!" she exclaimed.

Ahead of them, light could be seen breaking through the trees. They appeared to be coming to a clearing of sorts.

Jonah kept driving, merging through the trees and out into the open before finally coming to a stop.

"I don't think we're going to need that GPS anymore, the road ends here," Jonah said.

The road had indeed ended. In fact, the end of the road appeared to disappear into a lake.

Jonah put the car in park. Leaning forward on the steering wheel, he struggled to see anything ahead of him through the windshield.

Suddenly the navigation system sprung to life. "You have arrived," the electronic voice said.

Jonah looked around, expecting to see a hotel, restaurants, gift shop, or anything that resembled a haunted building. Instead, the GPS had delivered them to a dock on the edge of a lake, its horizon shrouded in mist.

"Are you sure you put in the address correctly?" Jonah asked Audrey.

She matched the invite up to the address on the screen. "Yeah, this is apparently where we are supposed to be," Audrey replied.

Jonah shut the door with a sigh, looking around at the rest of the group as if to see if anyone else had any answers as to where they were supposed to go. None of them did.

They each turned toward the lake. There wasn't much else to look at. At their backs was nothing but dense forest stretching out as far as the eye could see. And in front of them was the lake, its water looking dark and unforgiving. If one were to stare into its depths for too long, one may come to suspect that they've seen movement far below. They couldn't see much else. Everything in front of them was covered by a wave of fog that hid its contents from them. The fog started at the base of the water and soared until it melded with the sky thousands of feet up. There was no telling what was behind it.

As they watched, the fog seemed to drift closer and closer to them, soon it would be on the verge of swallowing them whole.

Ding, ding! Ding, ding!

From off in the distance came the sound of a bell tolling. The group looked around, trying to pinpoint where the sound was coming from. It tolled again, closer this time. It seemed to come from the direction of the lake.

The group of friends looked toward the mist, where a ripple began to travel through the surface of the lake. Jonah's eyes followed the ripple back to its source, where a large dark object was moving toward them through the fog. As it came closer, they were able to make out a large wooden boat. The sound of oars could be heard slapping the surface of the water.

The man rowing the boat ceased what he was doing and stood up, his shadowy figure towering over the lake. He wore a cloak that hid the top of his face, leaving only a bedraggled gray beard visible beneath. As they watched, he used the oar to guide the boat to the dock, sidling it right alongside before coming to a stop.

They each stared at the man, waiting to see who would make the first move.

Welcome To Nightmare Island

"Peterson party?" came a voice that seemed much too high-pitched to come from the man.

The group looked around at each other, confused looks on their faces.

"Peterson party?" came the voice again. Just then, a second man appeared from behind the man in the cloak. He was a frail man. Bespectacled and carrying a clipboard, he looked inquisitively at them, waiting for a response.

"That would be us," Jonah choked out. He coughed and tried again. "I'm Jonah Peterson."

The man pulled out a pocket watch, giving it a glance. "Right on time," he said coming to his feet. The boat began to wobble as he did so, and he quickly sat down again looking flustered. "It says here that you are staying with us for three days and three nights, is that correct?"

"That would be correct," Jonah exclaimed. "Where is the hotel, if you don't mind me asking?"

"Ah yes," the man said. "The hotel is on the island. It is only accessible by boat. Unfortunately, motorized vehicles are not allowed on Lake Sadness, so we are stuck traveling to the island on this." With that, the man waved to the boat beneath him with disgust.

"Right," Audrey said, giving the boat a once-over. "Can it hold all of us?"

Chapter Three

Twenty minutes later they were all crammed into the rowboat, shoulder to shoulder with their luggage on their laps.

"Right then," the man said, taking another glance at his pocket watch. He pushed his glasses up the bridge of his nose and turned to face them. "My name is Miles; I will be your tour guide for today." He looked at his clipboard before continuing. "The island was purchased several years ago by Maverick Knight, the most renowned demonologist in the world. Throughout his travels, Maverick faced some of the most vicious and horrifying demons the world had ever seen. He became wealthy after developing a way to capture the spirits of his travels and transport them away from the homes and villages they haunted. However, after capturing these spirits, he needed a place to put them to prevent the ghosts from terrifying the innocents. So, Maverick purchased this island to store the ghosts, and rigged it so they couldn't leave."

Jonah and his friends looked at each other, sharing grins. This guy was acting like ghosts and spirits were real. The group was used to this spiel. They had been to some of the most "haunted" places in the country and had never seen anything that they could justify as a "real" ghost. Likely, what was going to happen instead was they were going to find an island full of people dressed up as ghouls and goblins trying to scare them. Obviously not real, but still fun.

Not seeming to notice the snickers of the group, the man continued with his story. "After collecting some of the most terrifying spirits in the world, Maverick decided that he needed to share his experience with others, so he developed a bracelet that would allow the wearer to not be harmed while in the proximity of a demon. With the invention of this wristband, others would now be allowed to visit the island."

He reached underneath his seat and pulled out a box. Inside were five metal wristbands, with a glowing white strip through the middle of each. He passed one to each member of the group and they slipped them on one by one.

Jonah slid his bracelet upon his wrist, shivering as the cold metal touched his skin. He was able to get a better view of the wristband now that it was on his person. The white strip on the band seemed to be pulsing with energy.

Miles cleared his throat and spoke again in a more serious manner. "Do not for any reason take these bracelets off your wrists while on the island. Doing so could result in a painful, untimely death."

Jonah's friends grinned at each other. This guy was good.

The boat drifted further through the shroud of mist, which seemed to get thicker as they went. It became harder to see his friends who were sitting right next to him. The sounds of their voices even became harder to hear.

Then, an eerie chill passed through Jonah. It was as if the temperature had just dropped ten degrees in an instant. His friends seemed to notice it too, looking around at each other, their grins fading.

"Ah, yes, we must be close. The dead tend to give off a chill when you're near them." Miles said.

It felt like being underground. Hell, it *smelled* like being underground. A faint earthy scent permeated the air. Jonah could only imagine that this is what a grave must smell like.

As he watched, the mist began to dissipate and a large mass was coming closer and closer to them, becoming clearer as they went. Their eyes took in everything as the island revealed itself in the mist.

Suddenly, their jaws dropped.

Miles shifted in his seat, looking at the expanse behind him. Turning back to them he said, "Welcome to Nightmare Island."

Chapter Four

Standing on the dock, they tried to take in the sight before them. The main building seemed to be a gothic-style asylum with a village of supporting structures around it. It was very tall, casting the rest of the island in its shadow. Its moss-covered walls were made of cement thick enough to withstand an army. As their eyes traveled upwards, they settled upon the spires of the asylum. They were decked out in menacing gargoyles and were probably used as observation towers to keep a lookout for escaped patients.

"Of course, there's an asylum," Audrey said.

"That's one of the things about relocating ghosts. You can't just drop them off at a playground and hope that they stay put. They thrive in areas where death and hardship are common. And for the number of ghosts that Maverick was relocating, he needed an especially awful location," Miles said.

The island was deathly quiet but loud at the same time. Every noise they made seemed to echo throughout the village. Jonah stepped on a stick, freezing in place as the sound of it breaking reverberated against the buildings.

There was a sudden noise behind them. They jumped, turning to see the man on the boat hurriedly pushing off from the dock.

"Where is he going?" Jonah asked.

"He doesn't like to hang around. Those who live near the island tend to try to spend as little time near it as possible," Miles said looking back into the mist. "I don't blame them."

Jonah looked around hesitantly, shivering as a chill ran down his spine. The guy in the robe was terrifying to look at, and Jonah wasn't too keen on meeting whatever struck fear into that individual.

Mist floated through the buildings and puddled around their feet. The area was dark and desolate, even though it was still early. Jonah pulled out his phone to check the time.

"You're not going to have any service on the island," Miles said, glancing at Jonah's phone. "There's no way to call for help if you need it, and no one who would come if there was. The only way off the island is by that boat," Miles pointed over his shoulder at the boat growing smaller and smaller in the distance. "And it won't be back until the three days are over."

They watched as the fog swallowed up the boat. It looked as if nothing had even been there. The water was smooth as glass and dark as night.

"Let's go," Miles said, trudging off toward the buildings. The group followed somewhat reluctantly.

The sounds of their boots hitting the wet cobblestones reverberated off the walls of the buildings as they walked. The shadows in between each stone structure seemed to beckon to them as they moved forward. It made Jonah feel uneasy, almost as if they were being watched.

He glanced through the window of a small house as they walked by. It looked like whoever was living there left in a hurry. There were still dishes on the dining room table, its contents black with age. The house's occupants hadn't taken any of their stuff with them. The furniture was still covered in personal belongings, and picture frames still lined the mantle.

Welcome To Nightmare Island

"You said the spirits needed an especially awful place to be able to relocate them, what happened here?" Jonah said.

Miles hesitated before responding. "In the past, this island had been used to house an asylum for the criminally insane. Its occupants were known for especially heinous acts. The other buildings you see here were meant to support the asylum. To save from having to float everyone across the lake every day, houses were built to let the employees and their families live on the island. One day, during a particularly awful storm, the asylum lost power. The patients used that time to overpower the staff. Without power, the remaining staff couldn't radio for help from the mainland. The residents weren't prepared to evacuate all at once. Some got away on the few spare boats there were on the island. The rest, well, let's say they weren't so fortunate. Dozens of innocent people were hunted down with nowhere to go. They were all slaughtered."

The group blinked, taking in this information. Looking around, Jonah imagined people running through the streets, trying to find someplace to hide, being chased down by a group of insane, murderous individuals.

There it was again. The feeling like he was being watched. Jonah touched his hand to the back of his neck, feeling the hairs rise as he scanned the area. He didn't know if he was feeling the eyes of the people who died, or something much worse.

"Eventually, the patients were captured, and control was regained over the island. But nobody wanted to come back to work anymore. A few days later the authorities deemed the island unfit to house the asylum and it was shut down. The asylum and the surrounding buildings had been abandoned ever since," Miles said.

"Until I took over, that is," came a voice from behind them. It was a strong voice, spoken with great authority.

They turned around, seeing a tall, handsome man standing behind them. He wore his dark black hair slicked back on his head and walked with an air of confidence.

"I am Maverick Knight."

Chapter Five

"You may be wondering why I created this attraction," Maverick said. "It all started many years ago. I had a wife; Jennifer, and a daughter; Alice. I loved them very much. I wanted to spend the rest of my life cherishing their presence. Alas, it wasn't meant to be. Shortly after Alice's sixth birthday, they were both murdered while I was at work. I couldn't live with myself for not being there when they needed it most. I was supposed to protect them. I was supposed to keep the bad things away."

Jonah had unknowingly grabbed Audrey's hand, and he gave it a little squeeze. His breath had caught in his throat, and he had to remind himself to breathe again.

Maverick continued. "Being without my family has been unbearable, and I knew I had to find a way to see them again. I tried everything. Psychics, tarot cards, Ouija boards, and still nothing. I searched the globe studying the ways that other cultures used to try to contact the dead. With this knowledge, I became able to contact the other side. But it wasn't my family that I saw. It was much worse."

Audrey's hand squeezed Jonah's a little tighter.

"There are things on the other side that no man should see.

Welcome To Nightmare Island

Ghosts and demons of the most malevolent sort. Some of them still walked the earth and haunted some of the cultures that I visited. I couldn't stand by and let these innocent people get hurt, so I used my training as an engineer and developed a device that would allow me to capture these spirits and transport them away from these troubled areas. But I needed someplace to put them."

Maverick went on, "I remembered the stories of this island being told to me as a child, and I set out to find it."

He took a moment to appraise his surroundings, taking in all the old buildings around him.

"I bought the island, and then I let the ghosts loose in specialized areas around the property. Now, visitors to the island can experience what it's like to see a ghost in real life. To experience true terror for the first time in their lives. But don't worry, you'll be perfectly safe if you don't take those wristbands off." With this, Maverick pointed to a wristband that adorned his own wrist.

Jonah looked down at his hand, still intertwined with Audrey's. The light on their bands pulsed and they gave off a slight clang as they grazed each other.

"Miles here will show you all to your rooms. Get some sleep while you can. The tour begins at nightfall."

Jonah heard a cough and they all turned to face Miles once more. As he began speaking again, Jonah took a moment to glance back toward Maverick. Except, he wasn't there anymore. Jonah looked around, expecting to see him tagging along behind the group, but he was nowhere to be seen. He shrugged his shoulders, turning back to face Miles once again.

He was leading the group toward one of the larger buildings on the island. Though not quite as big as the asylum, this four-story building seemed to cast its shadow over the group even in the fog.

"This is the Sagamore Hotel," Miles said. "Its existence predates even the asylum. Early visitors to the island had the idea of making this into a resort, but things all changed when accidents began happening across the island. Several people died during the construction of some of the outlying buildings and the resort idea was abandoned. The only project completed at the time was the Sagamore Hotel."

Jonah looked up at the windows of the fourth floor. He saw a flurry of movement out of the corner of his eye, and he looked toward one of the windows at the far end. A curtain slowly moved back into place. Was somebody watching them?

He let his gaze rest on the window, waiting to see any other sign of movement. If there was somebody watching them from behind the curtain, eventually they would look through the window again, right?

He would've kept staring if it weren't for the hand that suddenly grabbed his shoulder.

Jonah jumped, spinning quickly on his heel to see Audrey standing there, a worried look upon her face.

"Are you okay?" Audrey asked. "You've been staring at the building for a while."

"I'm okay," Jonah said briefly.

"Did you see something?" she asked, looking over his shoulder at the building behind him.

"It was nothing. Probably just my imagination," Jonah said. He didn't want to frighten her over what may have just been the wind.

Miles was leading the rest of the group toward the hotel. They quickened their step to catch up.

The door to the hotel was a sight to see. It had a massive red door made from solid oak. The paint on the outside of the door was peeling so badly that the paint chips caught the falling leaves. There was something about the way this paint peeled that made Jonah think of scars. But the most fascinating piece of this door was the large iron door knocker in the center. It had the head of a gargoyle, its eyes seeming to look right into Jonah as he got closer.

Miles grasped the iron handles and pulled.

As soon as the door opened, they caught a whiff of something pungent. It was the kind of smell that all old buildings seemed to have; a musty scent that gave away the fact that the building hadn't been disturbed in years.

Miles reached around blindly along the walls. Finally, he found what he was looking for. He flipped a switch, and the lights slowly flickered on. The lights were housed in metal sconces on the walls, and they lit up things that hadn't seen light in ages. Tan and red wallpaper covered every flat surface, slightly yellowed from age and cigarette smoke. Spiders had cast their webs across the corners so thick that it seemed like the fog had made its way indoors.

"Doesn't this place have housekeeping?" Audrey asked.

"No such luck," said Miles with a grin.

He walked them through the lobby, where a brass chandelier hung in the center of the room. They passed some couches in the lobby, their leather dried out and cracked. A layer of dust coated everything in the room. A check-in desk stood at the end of the room, and the hotel's logo was plastered on the wall behind it, where one of the letters had apparently fallen off. The new logo read "The Sagmore Hotel."

After passing the desk, they took a turn down a hallway which led to the elevator.

Audrey took one look at the elevator and asked, "Do you expect us to go on that thing?"

Miles turned back to Audrey and smiled. "Yes. Yes, I do."

"Is it safe?" Audrey asked.

The elevator was ancient. Audrey had good reason to be concerned. This elevator may not have been used in the last century. Jonah highly doubted that the owners kept up yearly maintenance on the thing. The doors were plated in brass and molded to depict a lighthouse when the doors were closed.

Picking up a flashlight by the door, Miles stepped inside the elevator. The whole thing creaked as he did so, and they all waited in response to see if anything was going to happen. After a moment, Miles waved to them to join him. They did so reluctantly, each of them slowly stepping into the metal death trap. The elevator protested with every movement they made.

Once inside, Jonah took a moment to view his surroundings. Besides being in a creepy decrepit hotel, the elevator was quite beautiful. It was red with gold trim that flourished at each corner. He looked up to see his reflection staring back at him. There was a mirror that spanned the length of the ceiling.

Once they were all inside, Miles pressed the button to close the doors, which immediately banged shut with a resounding clash. They hesitated, listening to the sound of the crash echo through the elevator shaft and then each floor of the hotel. They waited another moment or two as the sound died away as if waiting to see if it woke up whomever or whatever may be living in the hotel.

The light in the elevator car wasn't that great, so Miles brought the flashlight up to the buttons to better see what he was doing. His fingers grazed against each number as he searched for the right floor number. Finally, his finger found its destination and he pressed the button for the third floor.

Suddenly everything seemed to swing into motion. The heavy silence of the hotel was broken as the humming of a motor echoed up the elevator shaft. The elevator seemed to shudder as it was shaken from the spot that held it for over a century. At last, with a loud groan, the elevator began to move upwards, shaking and creaking as it went.

Jonah looked over at Audrey. Her face was drained of color and her knuckles were white from the force of her grip on the brass banister. Apparently un-serviced, hundred-year-old elevators weren't her style.

They reached their floor and the elevator jolted to a stop, swaying slightly over the chasm that was the elevator shaft. Miles opened the gate and they all stepped out into the hall, which seemed almost identical to the one downstairs except for the rows of wooden doors on either side.

He showed each of them to their rooms, opening their door and beckoning inside. But before they walked in, however, he grabbed Jonah's shoulder.

"There are a few rules that you must abide by while in the Sagamore Hotel," Miles said. "Unless I come to get you, don't leave your rooms for any reason. Not if you hear or see anything strange. If you happen to hear your loved ones calling out to you, don't answer. It's not them. Unless you hear my voice, don't open your doors or windows. And for no reason at all should you visit the fourth floor."

Jonah glanced up at the ceiling, toward the fourth floor. He meant to ask him about it, but Miles wasn't standing next to him anymore. He stuck his head into the hallway, but Miles was nowhere to be found. Apparently, it was normal for the people who work on the island to just disappear without a trace. Jonah sighed and closed the door. He dropped their bags on the floor at the foot of the bed and began to unpack.

Their room consisted of a bed, wardrobe, and a closet in the far corner. An alarm clock stood on the nightstand next to the bed. An area rug took up most of the room. There was a very large black stain that adorned the center of the rug.

"I wonder when the last time these sheets were washed," Audrey said poking at the bedcover.

Jonah laughed and unpacked his bags. "I think I packed an extra set just in case." Finding the clean sheets, he threw them to Audrey and set about helping her make the bed.

Jonah couldn't help but wonder about the hotel rules. Why wouldn't they be allowed on the fourth floor? Maybe they hadn't finished the construction? Maybe the floors were rotted, and they didn't want them to fall through?

And what were the other rules? If he heard his loved ones calling, it's not them, so don't answer. Such a strange rule, why would he hear that? Audrey was in the room with him, and all his other loved ones were still back home.

Jonah walked over to the window. From up here you could see more of the island. Not much more, because the fog still hid much of everything. He looked out into the courtyard, and he thought he saw someone walk behind a building. Jonah focused his eyes on that spot but didn't see any movement. Jonah thought he must be losing his mind. He had traveled a long way and was tired and his eyes must have been seeing things. That had to be it.

Later that night, after they had finished unpacking, they laid down to try to get some sleep before the tour. It had been a long drive, and they expected to be awake most of the night.

Jonah fluffed his pillow up. He was exhausted. Being the driver on the way here, he had to be alert and keep his eyes on the road and therefore had no opportunity to rest his eyes during the drive like his passengers did.

He was right on the cusp of falling asleep when he heard it. His eyes shot open.

In Chuck and Annie's room, Annie had heard the noise too. She shook Chuck's shoulder vigorously to wake him up.

"Babe, wake up. I just heard something," Annie said.

"Go back to bed, it's probably just Kevin," Chuck said glancing at her with half-closed eyelids before rolling back over.

"The noise didn't come from across the hall, it came from upstairs," Annie said, exasperated.

Chuck grunted in acknowledgment, but he wasn't concerned enough to wake up.

That's when he heard it too. He shot up in bed, the sleep already gone from his eyes. "It sounded like it came from upstairs," Chuck said.

"That's literally what I just said," Annie, replied rolling her eyes.

Chuck jumped out of bed, quickly throwing his pants on. He listened intently for the noise to appear again. Suddenly he stiffened as the sound boomed from upstairs.

It sounded like chains rattling and dragging across the floor. He kept pace with the sound, walking through the hotel room trying to follow the path of the thing upstairs. Chuck imagined that the floor plan upstairs matched the one that they were currently on. He heard the thump, thump, thump of footsteps and tracked them leading out into the hall.

Chuck made a shush motion to Annie by placing his finger to his lips. He opened the door to the hallway, following the sound of the steps into the hall. Upon walking outside, he almost bumped into a shadowy figure standing right outside his door.

"What are you doing out here?" Chuck asked.

Jonah was standing in the dimly lit hall, still wearing his pajamas.

"I heard a noise and decided to check it out. Did you hear it too?" Jonah asked.

"Yeah, that's why I'm out of bed. What do you think it is?" Chuck asked.

"It sounded like whatever it is may be attached to a chain. I think it could be a dog," Jonah replied.

Suddenly a voice came from a door opposite the men in the hall.

"I think y'all should shut up. I'm trying to get my beauty sleep," Kevin said opening his door. He walked up to the other guys and said "What the hell are you guys doing out here? Don't you know what time it is?" He finished rubbing the sleep out of one eye and noticed the guys smirking at him. "What's so funny?" he asked.

"What are you wearing?" Chuck said with a grin.

Kevin was dressed in a matching set of blue pajamas, each adorned head to toe in yellow rubber ducks.

Kevin followed their gaze to his outfit, then brushed them off saying, "Say what you want fellas, these pajamas are some of the most comfortable things I've ever worn. If it weren't for you two making a racket out here, I would still be asleep in them."

The guys burst out laughing and were about to rag on Kevin further when another sound made them stop in their tracks. Except this time, it wasn't coming from above them.

This time it was coming from the end of the hall.

The guys all snapped their heads toward the elevator, which had randomly begun to hum mechanically as it moved. They could hear its machinery creaking in protest as it went, its sound echoing through the halls of each floor as it proceeded.

An audible ding could be heard as the doors opened down at the lobby. They paused a moment, hearing the doors close and the elevator began to rise again.

"Aren't we the only guests on the island?" Jonah said to the others.

"Us and whatever is upstairs," Chuck said.

They listened as the elevator shuddered to a stop again. They heard another ding as the doors opened once more, this time on the second floor. They listened intently to see if they could hear anyone exiting the elevator on the floor below them but heard nothing of the sort.

The doors closed once more, beginning the slow ride up to their floor.

"Maybe it's the tour guide. He probably forgot to tell us something. Or maybe he decided to start the tour early," Kevin suggested hopefully.

Each man clung to the frame of their hotel room doors with a white-knuckle grip as they waited to see what was going to step off the elevator.

The groaning and protesting of the elevator grew louder as it grew closer. Finally, it came to a stop.

Jonah waited with bated breath. The guys couldn't take their eyes off the doors. It felt like ten minutes had gone by but, it was probably only a few seconds.

The elevator dinged. Its doors slowly began to grind open. The guys forgot to blink while they waited for the elevator to reveal who it was.

The doors came to a stop. Jonah stood there staring. He took one step forward. Then another. He walked slowly up to the elevator, inspecting the inside.

It was completely empty.

"There's nobody here," he called back to the other guys. "Either somebody is pulling a prank and decided to press all of the buttons, or the elevator is just old and malfunctioning."

He walked back to Chuck and Kevin, who still hadn't moved from their doorways.

The elevator doors shut, and it began its slow trek back down to the lobby.

"Come on, let's get some sleep. The tour is going to begin in a few hours." Jonah said.

Chapter Six

Jonah awoke with a start. There was a rapping at their door. He heard a groan and looked over to see Audrey similarly awoken.

He threw off the covers, getting up to answer the door. Jonah swung it open to reveal an abashed-looking Miles. He was carrying a long flashlight and kept glancing over his shoulder nervously.

"It's time for the tour to begin," he said. He swung the beam of his light toward Audrey's direction. Seeing that Audrey was just getting out of bed, he grimaced and said, "Meet me in the courtyard in five minutes." Miles turned and shuffled down the hall.

Slipping on his jacket, Jonah stepped outside into the cold damp air. The fog here never seemed to lift. Something caught his eye around the corner of the building. He quickly turned his head to see a shadow moving in the fog, eventually disappearing without a trace altogether. As Jonah stared into the fog, the door shut loudly behind him as the rest of the gang filed out of the building.

Welcome To Nightmare Island

It may have just been a trick of the fog, or maybe his eyes haven't yet adjusted to the darkness, but he had to make sure.

"Miles, are we the only people on the island?" Jonah asked mildly.

"Oh, we are hardly the only beings on the island," Miles said.

There was something about the way he said "beings". It just didn't sit right with Jonah.

"Why do you ask?"

"I thought I saw something in the shadows," Jonah said.

Miles turned quickly, looking back over his shoulder to see if anything was there. Seeing nothing, he turned back to face them, a nervous look on his face.

"We ought to get a move on," Miles said. He began bustling through the courtyard like he was late for a meeting and the friends struggled to keep up.

There were gas lampposts spread out throughout the area that Jonah hadn't noticed on the way in. Their light shined feebly, not making a dent in the fog whatsoever. As they kept walking, he looked back to see the hotel completely swallowed up by the fog.

Eventually, they came upon a building that stood out from the rest. They stopped walking and stared up at the faded red cross on the front.

Miles turned on his heel to face them. "This is the infirmary," he said. "If you get hurt while on the island, I advise that you do not come here seeking help. The things you'll see behind these doors will wish to cause you harm. If you are wearing your wristbands that cannot happen. So, whatever you do, do not take them off."

Jonah looked at the building. It was built from bricks that had been chipped and worn away by years of storm damage. But that wasn't what caught his eye. What grabbed his attention were the windows. They seemed hastily boarded up, and some gaps could be seen behind the boards. Behind each gap in the boards, there were holes in the glass, and the edges of the glass were tinged with a dark substance. Upon further inspection, Jonah could see glass shards on the ground on the outside of the building, as if the window had been broken from the inside.

Miles led the way to the door, which was barred on the outside by a heavy board resting upon two steel brackets. With a grunt, he lifted the board from its place, and Jonah noticed that the imprint of the steel brackets was grooved into the board as if applied by a large amount of force. Miles placed the board against the wall, then went back to the door. He took a deep breath, and then swung it open.

Immediately they were greeted with the worst smell imaginable. Jonah was pretty sure something died in this building and then the carcass was left to rot after all these years. Not just because of the smell, but also because of the hundreds of flies that swarmed around them as they made their escape through the open door.

Jonah hesitated for a moment, taking in one last gulp of fresh air before letting the door close behind him. He had to take a moment to let his eyes adjust to the darkness. What little light he could see was coming through the cracks in the boarded-up windows.

Miles smacked his flashlight against his palm, willing it to get brighter. Surprisingly enough, it seemed to work, and he was able to alleviate the darkness somewhat.

Jonah wished he hadn't done that.

The sight that greeted them in the infirmary was horrifying. There were trails of blood leading throughout each room as if multiple bodies had been dragged around the building.

Jonah glanced at Miles's face, which seemed more nervous than usual. He caught Jonah looking and then changed his features, becoming stone-faced.

"Right, we better get going," Miles said leading the way. With his flashlight outstretched in front of him, he led them down the hall to a stairwell. The stairwell was covered in bloody bare footprints.

Glancing down at the bloody footprints, Jonah could see the light of his flashlight dancing in the pool of red.

The blood was fresh. Whoever had made these tracks was still here.

Welcome To Nightmare Island

Making it to the top of the flight of stairs, they were greeted by a throbbing bluish glow. They walked deeper down the hall, the light growing brighter as they went. The friends turned around a corner and saw what the source of the light was.

They had entered a large room, possibly the hospital's cafeteria. Stretching from one side of the room to the other was a long blue light that formed a square. The light was pulsing and matched the light on their wristbands.

Though the pulsing band of light on the ground was unusual, it wasn't the light that made the entire group stop in their tracks. Inside the square of light were two ghosts.

"Ahem," Miles coughed as he began to speak again. His grip on his clipboard left him white-knuckled as he tried to tear his eyes off the ghosts long enough to read the contents of his notes. "The first two ghosts on our tour are Bertha and the child. These two are possibly the least harmful ghosts you will see on the island, depending on the circumstances."

None of them seemed to be paying too much attention to his speech. They were too stunned by what was in front of them. Inside the square of light was a huge woman dressed in the garb of a stay-at-home mom from the fifties. She wore a tattered blue dress and a white apron, both of which were smattered almost entirely with blood. Her fire-red hair was unkempt and parts of it were matted to the side of her head with blood. Her angry blue eyes seemed to stare right through each of them as she took each new person into account. If he didn't know any better, Jonah would almost think she was sizing them up for a fight.

She took one giant step toward them, and they all in turn took one hasty step back. That's when they noticed the second ghost sitting on the floor behind her. It was a child who seemed to be about the age of three. His coveralls and striped tee shirt seemed to be similarly covered in blood. He paid no mind to the newcomers as he happily munched on a piece of raw meat clinging to a leg bone in his hand.

"When these two are together, they wouldn't harm a soul. These ghosts are perfectly content to go about their own business. However, if you happen to see the child by itself, know that its mother is close behind, and you are in ultimate peril. Bertha is extremely protective over the child, and if she sees you anywhere near him, she will not hesitate to rip you apart."

Bertha took another step between them and the child, her face teeming with anger. She was breathing heavily, her chest moving up and down rapidly as she inhaled the stench of the room. She bared her teeth at them, showing black and yellow stubs plagued with cavities.

"Are you sure that we are safe being in the same room with them?" Audrey stammered out. Her eyes never left Bertha while she spoke.

"You see that glowing line on the floor?" Miles asked. He pointed to the square of light surrounding the ghosts. "That light is giving off a signal that the ghosts cannot cross. The wristband we have given you earlier is giving off the same signal. Technically, you can walk right up to them and if you are wearing the wristband, they cannot touch you. However, I wouldn't recommend it. The pulsing light on the floor and your wristbands is connected to a signal coming from an orb under the island. It was created by Maverick to maintain control over the ghosts."

"Aren't ghosts supposed to be invisible?" Kevin piped up from the back. Miles turned to see Kevin standing at the back of the group. He raised his voice to be heard over the chewing coming from the ghosts, but he also made sure to put every other member of the group between himself and the hungry spirits.

"They can choose to take a solid or invisible form in the wild, however, the lines that we have put in place take away most of their supernatural abilities," Miles said.

He reached into a bin next to the wall nearby and pulled out a slab of raw meat. "The ghosts like to feed on raw flesh. If they don't receive their daily meal, they can get eccentric and become hard to handle." Miles threw the slab of meat across the room, where it landed with a sickening thud in front of Bertha. She snatched it up and immediately began to violently rip into it with her teeth, blood pouring down her chin as she did so. She was surprisingly quick for such a big woman.

"We should get a move on while these two are distracted," Miles said. He began to lead the group to a door on the other side of the room.

It took him a bit to gain their attention, as they were all still stunned at the fact that there were real ghosts in front of them. Not make-believe. Not teenagers dressed in costumes.

Real ghosts.

As they crossed the floor, Bertha's eyes bored into theirs, not missing a single movement even as she annihilated the meat in her hands.

As they exited the cafeteria into the hallway, leaving the stench of death behind them, Jonah could still picture Bertha's eyes.

He was sure he would never forget that sight for as long as he lived.

Chapter Seven

They stepped into the cold night air. Jonah took in a deep breath, inhaling the fresh air with a smile. It still smelled like a fresh grave outside, but he was happy to put the infirmary behind him.

"Right this way," said Miles. He held the flashlight in front of him and started along the cobblestone path. He didn't look back to see if they were following him. He didn't have to; they were all very eager to put as much distance between them and Bertha as possible.

Pretty soon a large black object could be seen in the fog. With a tinge of fear, Jonah realized that he knew what this building was. If Bertha and the child were the least dangerous ghosts on the island, he didn't want to know what was lurking in the dark depths of this building.

Miles reached the front door, turning on his heel to face them once more. "This is the insane asylum," he said. "This is home to some of the most vicious ghosts that Maverick has ever caught. Whatever you do, be sure to stay with the group. Do not leave the path that I lead you on. Doing so could result in you getting lost in the asylum, and many men have gone mad just trying to find a way out."

Welcome To Nightmare Island

"You're saying the ghosts in there are worse than Bertha?" Kevin asked incredulously. "On second thought, I think I left something important in the hotel room. I'm gonna go get it. I'll catch up with y'all later."

Kevin turned to leave. Jonah grabbed him by the back of the shirt and quickly turned him around. "You're not going anywhere," Jonah said with a smile. "This trip was as much your idea as it was ours. You're going to have to go through it with us. And there is no way we are splitting up in this place."

Grimacing at the exchange going on between Kevin and Jonah, Miles turned back toward the doors. He reached for the door handle, hesitating for a moment, before opening the big wooden door. Its hinges squeaked violently, creating a crescendo of echoes in the halls beyond.

They walked in silence through the halls of the asylum, listening to the sound of their footfalls on the tile floor. Jonah realized that he was holding his breath, struggling to listen for any sounds in the darkness.

Miles swung the beam of his flashlight over the walls as he went, finding landmarks to let him know where he needed to go. His light illuminated posters on the wall, yellowed with age and long forgotten. Signs from when the asylum had still been open, asking people to stand six feet apart, face forward, and stay quiet. One sign they passed caught Jonah's attention.

There was a splotch of red on the bottom left corner. In fact, there was a trail of red leading from the poster to the floor. Jonah followed the trail with his eyes, and what he saw made him stop in his tracks. There was a set of bloody handprints on the ground. But it didn't stop there. The blood trail started at the handprints and led all the way down the hall, to a set of double doors.

Miles, upon seeing Jonah pause, followed his gaze. Seeing the blood trail, he nodded. "Ah yes. What you are seeing are the remnants of the assault on the asylum. When the patients escaped, there wasn't anywhere for the asylum staff to go. They were hunted down in these very halls. Many of the bodies were never recovered. Those who weren't immediately slaughtered were captured and brought into many different areas in the building, where the patients decided to uh, experiment on them."

"What do you mean, experiment?" Chuck asked.

"The staff at this asylum were known to experiment with unorthodox methods of treatment," Miles said. "Electric shock therapy, deprivation of oxygen to the brain, and many other remedies to try to fix a patient's mental state. One doctor even believed that there was a part of the mental patient's brain that was inconsistent with the brain of that of someone normal, so if they could surgically remove that part of the brain..."

"Please don't finish that sentence," pleaded Kevin. He was always a bit squeamish once people started talking about medical terms.

"Yes, well as I was saying," continued Miles, "once the patients were free, they decided to use these unorthodox methods on the staff. Give them a taste of their own medicine, so to speak."

They all paused for a moment, imagining the torture that the people inside this building had to endure.

Miles went on. "Where we are headed next is..."

Please not behind those doors, please not behind those doors, Jonah thought to himself.

"Behind those double doors there," Miles finished.

Jonah cursed under his breath.

The group reluctantly followed the trail of blood through the double doors. None of them knew what to expect on the other side of those doors. Nothing could have prepared them for what they found.

They let the double doors swing behind them. They paused for a moment to take in the scene before them. The walkway opened into a room with black and white checkered floors. There were windows on either side of the room draped in lacey pink curtains. While this room seemed entirely out of place in a haunted asylum, it wasn't the curtains that caught everyone's eyes.

Welcome To Nightmare Island

In the center of the room stood a table with four chairs around it. Each chair was presently occupied. At the head of the table sat a man with his back turned to the group. However, he appeared to be having a tea party with the other occupants of the table. As the group drew closer, they could see that the other three occupants were dead.

The corpses at the table were all dressed in scrubs. One would assume that the nurses at the asylum had taken a moment to take a break and enjoy some tea. However, upon closer inspection, you would notice the sunken eyes and the lopsided heads with sagging skin.

The man at the table raised his teacup to the others, who naturally, did not move an inch.

"I would like to make a toast to all you fine gentlemen. Thank you for taking the time out of your busy schedules to come have tea with me. It gets so lonely here, and it means so much to me to have your company present." Turning to the corpse on his right he said "Gerald! How are the wife and kids? I trust they're doing splendidly. Here, let me help you with that." He grabbed the teacup in front of the corpse and proceeded to raise it to "Gerald's" mouth. He suddenly snatched the cup away from the corpse. "Woah, woah, not so fast! If I didn't know any better, I would assume you are trying to get out of here as soon as possible. Do I not please you with my company? Are you ashamed of me? Well, consider my feelings well and truly hurt, Gerald."

With that, he threw the cup to the ground where it shattered to pieces. The sudden clatter startled Audrey, who squeaked before quickly cupping her hands to her mouth. But it was too late.

The man swiveled in his seat, turning to face the group. "Gents, it appears we have company. Apparently, they haven't learned that it is rude not to knock."

"This is Jones Jepsen," said Miles. "Jones was a homicidal maniac who decided he wasn't going to let death stop him from torturing the living."

"At your service," Jones said taking a bow. He was wearing a velvet trench coat and his coattails brushed the ground as he did so. He had shoulder-length black hair that looked like it hadn't been washed in... ever. Perched upon his head was a bowler hat, which he pitched forward and gazed out at them from underneath. "How rude am I? I have guests, I should have offered you all a seat. Gerald, please get up." Jones stood patiently while facing the group, twiddling his fingers behind his back. He didn't have to look behind him to know that the carcass of "Gerald" was not moving.

In the space of an instant, Jones seemed to lose his patience. He turned, pulling a large mallet from within his trench coat, and swung it with all his might. The end of the mallet connected with the skull of the corpse with a sickening thwack, which sent its head flying off its host. The head flew across the room, bits and pieces of face falling off midair as it spun, before finally hitting the wall nearby. The head exploded, splattering brains and skull fragments across the pink curtains.

Jones kicked the body of the corpse off the seat before beckoning the friends over to the chair. "Please have a seat," Jones said with a huge grin.

"I think I'm going to pass on that," Kevin said, his eyes dancing between Jepsen and the splattered skull on the wall.

"Suit yourself!" said Jones. He threw the mallet against his shoulder and skipped over to them, his head tilting from left to right as he went. From his demeanor, you wouldn't have known that he had just blown apart the body of a corpse. In fact, he seemed absolutely delighted to see the group of tourists in front of him.

Suddenly, he stopped in place, his mood changing altogether. He looked down at the floor, seeing the pulsing blue line that divided his side of the room from theirs.

"Say doc, when are you gonna turn this blue thingy off and give me a tour of the place?" Jones said.

Miles looked at Jones with a stern face and said, "If it was up to me, I'd move your cell to the bottom of the lake."

Welcome To Nightmare Island

Jones paused for a long while, then his face cracked and he began to cackle, throwing his head back to let his crazed laugh reverberate off the ceiling. "That's funny, doc," he said.

Miles turned back to face the group. "When Jones was alive, he would go on endless rampages, traveling from town to town and murdering victims at random. But he didn't like to just kill people. That would have been too simple. Jones here thrived on finding different ways to make his victims scream. If you can think of a way to torture someone, odds are Jones has tried it."

Jonah looked back at Jepsen. Currently, he was dragging his mallet along the invisible barrier created by the pulsing light, as if trying to find a weak spot that he could crawl through.

Miles continued, "When the authorities finally caught up to Jones, they found him playing in the blood of his victims. He was tried and ultimately put to death."

He took a moment to look over his shoulder as if to make sure the barrier was still holding up against Jepsen's queries. "Apparently, that wasn't the last time the world would feel the effects of Jones Jepsen. On the anniversary of his death, people began to report gruesome murders reminiscent of when Jones was tormenting the town. His spirit had decided to come back from the dead to haunt the living once more."

Growing impatient, Jepsen decided to give up trying to find a gap in the barrier. Instead, he decided that the best call to action would be to smash his way through. He began to swing wildly at the barrier with his mallet, causing a field of blue to appear every time he struck it. He struck the barrier again and again, causing a sound like a church bell to go off every time he connected. However, it was of no avail. Jepsen wasn't making any progress on the barrier. Every time he swung, the mallet would bounce off harmlessly, and after a moment even the blue areas that appeared after he struck it would seem to heal itself. It was as if he hadn't hit the invisible barrier at all.

Miles had stopped talking. Everyone in the group couldn't help but stare at Jepsen as he went about his relentless tirade on the barrier.

"Let." *Bang.* "Me." *Bang.* "Out!" screamed Jepsen as he struck the wall repeatedly.

Miles, upon seeing the barrier hold firm, turned back to the group. "Maverick began to hear tales of a ghost coming back to murder the members of the town, so he knew he had to check it out. He captured Jones Jepsen, ridding the town of his presence, and brought his spirit here to rot for as long as he decides to be on this side. Jepsen is free to go back to hell whenever he pleases, but he seems to have a vendetta to kill more people before he's ready for retirement."

Jepsen had apparently tired of swinging his mallet, seeing no promising results. This, however, combined with the story of his capture and imprisonment, seemed to anger him even further. He stormed about his side of the room. Grabbing the teacups, he threw them one by one at the members of the group, who flinched as the cups smashed to bits on the barrier in front of them. He flipped the table across the room, then picked up the bodies of the corpses and flung them against the wall.

"He's going to go on like this for a while. Jepsen likes to throw fits when he doesn't get his way. We should leave now and stop giving him the attention he craves," Miles said.

As the group began to walk out of the room, Jonah looked back at Jepsen. His head was tilted down, breathing heavily. He looked out from beneath his cap to meet Jonah's gaze. Donning a wicked grin that bared all his teeth he said, "I'll be seeing you soon. Just wait, I will see you soon enough."

The group made their way through the dark passages. Miles guided them through using only the light from his flashlight. Jonah tried to keep up with the turns that they were taking, but it wasn't long before he lost track. They kept moving, down passage after passage, until Jonah thought that Miles must certainly be lost, and they would be trapped forever in the darkness of the asylum.

Welcome To Nightmare Island

Miles led them down a flight of stairs before finally coming to a halt in front of another pair of double doors. These had a square glass window inlaid in the top half of each door.

He turned back to face the group. "Welcome to the morgue," he said.

Chapter Eight

Immediately upon opening the doors, they were met with a familiar smell. A familiar, awful smell.

Covering her face with her shirt, Annie wheezed, "Are there dogs down here?"

They had been greeted by the smell of wet dog, so pungent and overwhelming that it became hard to take a breath. The group had to practice taking smaller breaths to avoid sucking in too much of the foul-smelling air, which surely would have made them vomit.

Jonah thought to himself, there must be a hundred dogs down here. That's the only possible excuse for a smell this bad.

Though it was hard to discern with the fact that they were trying not to breathe, the air was tinged with the smell of something else that they hadn't noticed at first. Were there more than just dogs down here?

They turned a corner, and the answer nearly bit their faces off.

"Bark bark, bark, bark!"

Once they rounded the corner, they found themselves face to face with a vicious group of dogs. Their mouths dripped with saliva as they snapped and snarled, desperately trying to get their jaws around the intruders.

Jonah looked into their eyes, and he could see no remorse, no fear, nothing that would hold them back once the dogs managed to catch their prey.

Upon further inspection, there appeared to be something off about these dogs, aside from the part where they wanted to rip the throats out of the group members.

It appeared that chunks of their bodies were missing as if they had deteriorated. The skin and fur in some places had decomposed, and in many areas, the flesh barely clung to the bone. Half of the flesh on the face of one dog was entirely missing, and you could see where its fangs connected to the rest of its skull.

These dogs weren't alive.

Miles reached into a bin near him and grabbed a slab of raw meat. He picked a spot on the other side of the room and tossed the meat toward that area.

Immediately the dog's eyes, or what remained of them, followed the meat as it arced across the room, landing with a sickening thud.

It happened so fast that if Jonah had blinked, he would have missed it.

The dogs launched themselves at the meat, ripping and tearing at it with their teeth. If one dog got too close to another, they would snap and bark at each other until one of the dogs backed down.

It wasn't until the dogs were safely on the other side of the room that they noticed the other ghost in the room.

He was a big burly man. The veins on his arms danced as his oversized muscles moved. The man's face was pocked with scars, including one jagged gash which stretched from his forehead through his left eye and down to the center of his cheek. The eye in question was white as a bone, whereas the other one was solid black.

The man was holding a set of leashes in each hand, each of which connected to a dog. The veins in his arms jumped here and there as the dogs struggled against their restraints.

Though the dogs seemed distracted by their meal, the man's one good eye bored into the friends.

"This is the Huntsman and his hounds," Miles said. "The Huntsman is from the deep south. Back in his prime, the Huntsman trained hunting dogs. The only thing was, his dogs weren't trained to hunt animals. These dogs were trained to hunt people. The Huntsman lived during the days of slavery, and when the slaves escaped from the plantation, the owners would hire him and his dogs to bring back their bodies."

The Huntsman's eye moved slowly from person to person as Miles spoke. It was almost like he was daring them to move, and then he would sic the dogs on them.

"Years had passed since the Huntsman had died. Then the locals started reporting the sounds of dogs barking at night. Then animals began to go missing. Cats, dogs, livestock. The townspeople blamed all of this on a rising coyote population. So, one day the town organized a coyote hunt. Twenty men went out searching for coyotes, but what they met instead were the Huntsman and his hounds. The men tried to kill the hounds, but you can't kill something that's already dead. None of the men were ever seen alive again. The dogs ripped the men to shreds and then ate the shreds."

The Huntsman trained his one good eye on Jonah, and he felt his blood run cold. He felt like the Huntsman was looking into his soul, like he was sizing him up to see what kind of fight he would hold up against his dogs.

Just then, Jonah saw movement out of the corner of his eye. The dogs had finished their meal.

Sucking down the last morsel of food, the dogs turned their attention to the guests. They bared their teeth, snarling once more. They were still hungry.

Jonah remembered a fact he learned about dogs years ago. Most dogs don't know when to stop eating. They will keep stuffing their face even after they're sick.

At that moment, the Huntsman let go of the leashes. In a split second, the dogs leaped into action, racing toward the guests at lightning speed.

Just when they thought that they would all die down here in the jaws of these vicious beasts, the dogs encountered an obstacle. They ran into the invisible barrier, bouncing off it and falling backward against the floor.

But the dogs wouldn't give up. They saw their prey and saw nothing in front of them preventing them from getting to their prey. So, they tried again and again, each time getting angrier and snapping their jaws harder and harder. The sound of their barking became almost deafening, and Jonah couldn't hear himself think.

"I think it's time that we go!" Miles screamed over the noise of the hounds. He led the way toward the exit.

Jonah snuck one look back over his shoulder as he went. The Huntsman called his dogs back to his side with a flick of his wrist, and together the Huntsman and his hounds watched him go.

Chapter Nine

Miles led the way back through the hotel. The group of friends walked dazedly through the halls, seemingly stunned into silence by the events that had occurred that night. They had come here expecting people dressed in costumes to jump out from dark corners and go boo. What they found was much worse. They had seen ghosts. Like real ghosts, not men dressed in sheets trying to scare you, but the real thing.

Seeing actual ghosts changed their whole perspective on life. It was fun for the group to watch movies that made them jump or pay to see haunted attractions where they didn't know what was lurking around the corner. It was fun for them because at the end of the day, they knew that it wasn't real. They knew that when the haunted attraction was all over, they would be able to go back home to their beds safe and sound and reminisce about the fun times they had.

Nightmare Island changed their perspective entirely. Ghosts were real. Meaning that all the times they went to places that were supposedly haunted, they could have been met with an actual ghost. In the wild, not behind a barrier like on the island. Living a lifestyle

Welcome To Nightmare Island

where they visited haunted places from time to time could get them killed.

Strangely, here on Nightmare Island, which was full of some of the worst ghosts imaginable, they had never felt safer. They felt safe because here there was a system that protected them from getting harmed by ghosts. But now they feared going home. Home is where the ghosts were that didn't have anything preventing them from attacking the living.

They had stopped in front of the elevator. Miles took a moment to glance at his watch. Stiffening, he said, "I have somewhere I need to be right now. I trust you all can find your way back to your rooms?"

Jonah nodded. Kevin on the other hand seemed fearful.

"You're just gonna leave us here?" Kevin said. "What if we run into a ghost on the way to our rooms? What are we supposed to do? Fight a ghost?"

Miles lifted his wrist, showing us the pulsing band. "As long as you are wearing this, the ghosts can't get to you." He backed away, disappearing hurriedly into the darkness.

Kevin stared in the direction that Miles went, apparently horrified that their guide had left them alone on a haunted island full of ghosts.

The whole group jumped as a loud ding echoed throughout the room. The elevator had finally arrived to take them back to their rooms. The age-old mechanisms shrieked as the doors ground open.

As the group stepped inside the elevator, they breathed a sigh of relief, cast in the dim light provided by the small elevator light above them. They felt relatively safe in the rickety old elevator as opposed to the outside world where the ghosts were. They could finally relax and joke around somewhat.

"You're just gonna leave us here?" mocked Chuck in a high-pitched voice.

"Oh, now you got something to say?" Kevin said. "Now that you're safe and sound in an elevator? Well, I'll tell you what, you ain't safe from me in here!"

The boys began playfully shoving each other around. In doing so, Kevin barreled into Chuck's legs, knocking him against the wall. For his part, Chuck tossed Kevin aside like a teddy bear. Kevin was no match for the ex-football player turned police officer. Kevin went stumbling backward, his back landing against the elevator buttons. When he came away, the buttons for all the floors were lit up.

"Now see what you did?" Kevin exclaimed to Chuck. "Now we have to spend even more time on this death trap."

The elevator began to stop on every floor. Since they were still on the first floor, the doors reopened, leaving Annie repeatedly pressing the close doors button. They felt the elevator shift and grind as it moved to the second floor. The doors squealed open, showing a floor plan like their own. Again, Annie was left pressing the close door button excessively.

"I wouldn't keep doing that if I were you," Audrey said. "This elevator is ancient; you don't know how the hardware is going to react to having too many commands at once."

Annie stuck out her tongue playfully at Audrey, then pressed the button one more time. The doors screamed shut once again, and the elevator began to rise toward the third floor.

Except, it didn't stop there. It rose for twice the amount of time that it was supposed to. The numbers at the top of the door lit up floor 3, but the elevator kept inching upwards. That's when they realized that it was going to the fourth floor.

Annie's face paled as she watched the numbers light up. Miles said there was something horrible on the fourth floor, and she wasn't trying to find out what it was tonight. She began pressing the 3 button feverishly, her eyes going between the button and the lit-up numbers at the top of the door. "Come on, come on! Work, God dammit!" She gave up on the 3 button and began to press every button. One, two, door open, door close. She pounded every button trying to prevent the elevator from rising. Finally, she pressed the emergency stop button and the elevator shrieked to a stop.

Welcome To Nightmare Island

Annie took a deep breath, steadying herself now that the elevator wasn't going to the fourth floor.

That's when they heard the ding. The group held their breath as the elevator doors began to slide open.

The doors opened to reveal that they had stopped mid-floor. Most of the open doorway was filled by a concrete wall, but at the top of the doorway, just above eye level, it opened slightly onto the fourth floor.

The group stood stock still, waiting to see if anything was there. The electricity must not be turned on for this floor. It was very dark, but they could just see the faint outlines of certain objects in the moonlight coming from the window of one of the rooms.

Suddenly, they saw shadows moving toward the end of the hall. Jonah couldn't quite see what it was, and his curiosity got the better of him. He reached his hands onto the sill of the next floor, trying to pull himself up to get a better view of the fourth floor. In doing so, he changed the amount of weight in the elevator, and it shifted in place, groaning loudly in protest of his movement. The sound reverberated down the hall. Jonah stopped moving instantly. At that moment he was pretty sure he forgot how to breathe. The whole group stood completely still, staring at the shadow to see if it heard the noise.

Immediately the shadow began moving in their direction. Slowly at first, but then it began to pick up speed. It was running closer and closer down the hall toward them. They could only see the bottoms of its feet but that was enough.

Jonah dropped to the floor of the elevator and began pressing buttons feverishly. Annie covered her face in the corner while the rest of the group joined Jonah in trying to press every button possible to get the elevator moving again. They could hear the thing getting closer, whatever it was. There was a loud metallic sound that seemed to scrape the ground as it ran, and they could hear its deep, ragged breathing.

Finally, just as the thing was about to reach them and Jonah felt his heart was going to burst from the sheer terror of it all, the doors slammed shut and the elevator began moving again.

The elevator arrived at the third landing, and they all tumbled out onto the floor, breathing hard.

Jonah reached desperately into his pockets, searching for something. His eyes were wild as he pawed at himself. Audrey saw him and reached into his pocket, drawing out his inhaler. He took it from her gratefully and took two deep pulls from it as he tried to catch his breath again.

"Next time I'm taking the stairs," Chuck said.

"What the hell was that thing?" Annie asked. She wasn't usually one to curse, so she must have been extremely shaken up to get this out of character.

"I don't know," Jonah said. "But I'm not going back up there to find out."

Chapter Ten

Jonah knew the moment that they got back to their rooms that they weren't going to be sleeping that night.

Ghosts were real. Today the group had seen some of the most horrifying specters that they or any living person had ever laid eyes on. The ghosts were truly terrifying to look at, and he kept seeing their faces every time he closed his eyes. His mind played a loop of Jepsen's last words to him. "I'll be seeing you soon. Just wait, I will see you soon enough."

What did that mean? Did Jepsen really believe he had a shot of getting out of his cage? And if he did, was this little wristband enough to prevent a homicidal ghost from tearing him apart limb by limb?

Furthermore, what was the thing lurking on the fourth floor? Was it the thing whose eyes Jonah had constantly felt watching him?

He thought about their time in the elevator. A few more moments and whatever was up there could have gotten to them easily. They probably didn't have too much reason to panic the way that they did, there was only a few inches of space between the floor and the opening of the elevator. There was no way that anything could have fit through that.

Devin Cabrera

But the sight of the shadow running toward them in the darkness still chilled him to the bone.

What nasty ghost did Maverick decide to stick on the floor above them? The island was big. There wasn't any other building to put it in? He had to place it right above where they slept?

Jonah's mind kept racing with unanswered questions.

Obviously, the hotel guests had to be safe. All the ghosts on the island were trapped behind their own barriers keeping them from escaping and murdering everything in sight. Plus, each of the guests were wearing a wristband that was supposed to act as a second barrier against the ghosts.

Jonah looked down at his wrist, twirling the band around absent-mindedly as he thought. Then he stopped twirling, his heart racing.

Jonah thought back to the elevator. Looking out onto the fourth floor, had he seen a barrier? Pacing around the room, he tried as hard as he could to remember. Of the light that there was, most of it seemed to come from moonlight. Was there a blue light correspondent to having a barrier? Or had he been too scared to notice it?

He stopped pacing. If there wasn't a barrier, what was keeping the thing upstairs from coming down to the third floor and murdering them all in their sleep?

Jonah was distracted from his thoughts by Audrey walking into the room. He decided that if they were going to stay here for three days, they were going to have to get some sleep.

Jonah didn't know when it happened, but apparently sometime during his restless thoughts he had ended up falling asleep. He glanced over to see Audrey asleep on the bed beside him. He smiled. She looked so peaceful sleeping there. For a moment he had almost forgotten the events of the night they just had. He would have fallen back asleep if he hadn't noticed the light.

Jonah blinked slowly, trying to make sure his sleep riddled eyes weren't deceiving him. No, it was still there.

Welcome To Nightmare Island

Jonah sat up in his bed.

There was light coming in from under the closet door.

Had Audrey left the closet light on last night? Jonah couldn't remember. To be honest, he didn't know if he had even noticed that they had a closet to begin with.

Sighing to himself, Jonah knew that his mind wouldn't allow him to fall back asleep knowing that a light was on. He pushed his covers aside and began to walk toward the closet door.

Then he saw something that made him hesitate.

There were shadows moving in the light cast under the door of the closet. Somebody was in there.

Maybe it was one of the guys trying to play a prank. Yes, that had to be it. He walked over to the door. Stopping just in front of it, he called out, "I know you're in there, you're not going to scare us."

He waited. Hearing no response, he grabbed the door handle and pulled, getting ready to scold whichever one of the boys was lurking in their closet.

But there was nobody there.

Jonah pushed the hanging clothes aside. Surely, he had just seen someone moving in the light from the closet. He crouched down, placing his face to the ground he looked underneath the row of clothes to see if he could see the persons feet.

Nothing.

Chalking it up to his eyes playing tricks on him, Jonah shut off the closet light and closed the door.

He began walking back to his bed when something made him stop in his tracks.

A beam of light was reflecting on the wall in front of him. He turned around, seeing that the closet light had turned back on.

"What the hell?" Jonah murmured.

He began to walk back toward the closet door.

Was it faulty wiring? This place was old, so it wasn't out of the question for its wiring to be bad.

He stopped in front of the door, about to turn the knob again when he thought he heard something.
Jonah paused for a moment. What was that?
He placed his ear to the door, listening for a moment.
Nothing. Silence.
And then, boom!
There was a loud bang as Jonah felt something slam against the door.
He rushed back away from the door, holding his face where he had just felt the impact. Looking down, he saw two shadows in the light coming from beneath the closet door.
Someone was standing on the other side.
Boom!
The door was rocked again by another loud bang. Jonah turned his head to see if Audrey had been awoken by the commotion. She hadn't moved a muscle.
Bang! It came again.
Jonah decided that he needed to know what was on the other side of the door. He reached into his pocket, pulling out his inhaler and taking two puffs before proceeding. He allowed himself a moment to catch his breath, then the air was rocked by another bang. Steeling himself, Jonah took out his phone. Opening the front facing camera, Jonah kneeled in front of the door and slowly slid the phone underneath.
What he saw frightened him to his core. Looking into the screen, Jonah saw a huge ghost. It was probably the size of three men put together. Its biceps were the size of cinder blocks and veins popped out from almost every inch of visible skin.
Bang!
Jonah could see what the noise was now.
The giant ghost was holding a man's body. He guessed that it was the body of one of the former nurses here, as he was wearing scrubs from head to toe.

Welcome To Nightmare Island

The ghost had palmed the man's face like a basketball and was repeatedly smacking it against the closet door.

Bang! The ghost slammed the man's head against the door once more, his limp legs bouncing harmlessly against the door just moments after.

Jonah stifled a scream.

The ghost stopped moving, seeming to have heard the slightest sound that Jonah made. His oversized neck rippled as his head turned to look down at the phone.

He felt the full weight of the ghost's eyes bare down upon him through the camera lens.

Jonah bolted. Grabbing his phone, he ran across the room to the bed.

He grabbed Audrey's shoulder, trying to wake her up.

"Come on, wake up! We have to go! There is something in our closet!" Jonah screamed.

He shook her again and again and oddly he received no response on her end. Puzzled, he grabbed her shoulder and turned her over.

Jonah screamed.

Audrey's eyes stared blankly at the ceiling; her throat was slit open. He let go in shock, her body falling limply back to the bed.

Jonah turned, just as the closet door crashed open and...

He woke up.

Jonah sat upright in bed, panting like a dog. His clothes were drenched in sweat. He turned to look at the closet, which seemed... normal. Suddenly remembering he grabbed Audrey's shoulder and pulled her over to face him.

"Ow!" Screamed Audrey through half closed eyes. "You sure know how to wake a girl."

Jonah breathed a sigh of relief. It was all a dream. But just to be sure, he got up and checked the closet.

There was nobody in the closet. No giant ghosts. No marks left on the inside of the closet door. It was just a dream.

It was daytime. Or rather, it was afternoon. Between being tired from the drive and trudging around the island all night, they had been so tired that they had slept through most of the day.

The group decided to check out the grounds before the ghost tour continued that night.

They followed the cobblestone path in front of the hotel. Stopping here and there to remark on a particularly spooky building, they soon stumbled on something they thought to be out of place on an island as creepy as this.

They came to a stop on the sidewalk, tilting their heads back to see. Towering over them was a huge lighthouse. It was white with red stripes, and the top contained a room full of windows, where Jonah guessed was where the light came from. At the base of the lighthouse there were boulders the size of minivans, set in place to keep the waves from crashing into the lighthouse too hard. It seemed totally out of place amongst the buildings filled with ghosts.

"Let's go inside," Chuck said.

Kevin looked at him dumbfoundedly. "Every building that we've been inside on this island was full of ghosts and dead things. Now you want to go inside without any supervision, in a building that we've never been in, regardless that there may be a man-eating demon inside?" Kevin said.

"Yes," Chuck said grinning at Kevin.

"I think it's pretty," Annie said as she walked toward the lighthouse.

"Besides, if there is something in there, we still have these, right?" With that, Chuck held up his wrist and shook it. The wristband spun around for a second, its pulsing as bright as ever.

Kevin grumbled some more, but ultimately, he agreed.

The group walked toward the lighthouse. Once they were right up next to it, they could see a set of rusty iron stairs leading to a door built into the side.

They began to climb the stairs. Jonah, who had maintained a firm grip on the railing as he went, pulled his hand away with some paint chips. This place, like any other on this island, was falling apart.

Welcome To Nightmare Island

Annie reached the door first, and she gave the handle a turn.

The door didn't budge.

"It's probably rusted shut. The door most likely hasn't been used in ages and needs to be forced open," Chuck said.

Chuck, who had probably busted open countless doors during his career as a cop, beckoned for everyone to move away from the door. Then, using the limited amount of space the stairwell landing offered him, he ran forward and threw his shoulder into the door. It opened with a bang, and as it bounced off the wall behind it, it sent a shower of paint chips down onto Chuck's shoulders.

Brushing his shoulders off, Chuck said, "That should do it."

Once their eyes adjusted to the darkness, the room began to take shape before them. Inside there was circular room. To one side there was a stash of spare equipment needed to let the lighthouse run. On the other side there stood a bed and a nightstand, probably placed there from the last time a lighthouse keeper was needed.

Jonah let the door shut behind him. After looking around the room, he had to acknowledge something unexpected about the room. It appeared to be lived in.

The blankets on the bed appeared to be mussed up, and there was a notepad on the nightstand. A pair of men's slippers lay at the foot of the bed.

Jonah got a good whiff of the air. It wasn't as stale as the air in every other building on the island.

He walked over to the notepad on the nightstand. Turning it over, it appeared to contain a list of chores.

He didn't know if this had been left here since the last lighthouse keeper was here, or if somebody was living here. Who would be crazy enough to live on an island like this?

Just then, they heard a loud noise from above them.

Jonah dropped the notepad on the nightstand and went over to stand by Audrey.

Each of them stared at the ceiling, listening for any other sounds of movement.

"Maybe there's an open window up there," Annie said. "Maybe there's a window open and the wind is blowing things around."

"Or maybe they stowed another ghost up here and we showed up early to the tour," Kevin said.

Another bang came from above, and the group seemed to flinch all at once.

"Shall we take a vote on whether or not we should leave right now?" Audrey said.

"Aye," the group said in unison.

Kevin led the way back to the door. He pulled on the handle, but the door didn't budge.

"Let me try," Chuck said.

"I don't need your help," Kevin retorted. "I'm a grown-ass man, I can open a door by myself.

He proceeded to grip the door handle with both hands, pulling with all his might. When the door still didn't move, he propped his foot against the wall and tried to leverage all his weight into opening the door. It hadn't moved an inch.

Huffing to himself, he backed away from the door. He looked in Chuck's general direction and swung his hand toward the door as if to say, "By all means."

Chuck walked up to the door and tugged at the handle. It didn't budge. For some reason, he seemed absurdly confused by this. Normally he would be able to open something like this. Was it locked? He checked the locking mechanism. Nope. If he were to apply enough force it should open. Using both hands he pulled until he was red in the face.

It wasn't going anywhere.

They heard another bang coming from upstairs.

"I guess if we can't find a way out of the front door, then we have to find another way," Jonah said.

The group searched around the room, looking through closets and scanning the ground for trap doors. But they came up empty-handed.

Welcome To Nightmare Island

As one, they looked toward the stairs to the upper landing.

"I guess the only way out is up," Annie said.

Chuck led the way, pushing Annie behind him. They slowly inched their way up the spiral staircase. Chuck stepped as quietly as he could, trying not to make a sound on the metal steps. He made it to the top step, and a confused look appeared on his face.

Jonah followed up behind him, and he too was mystified.

They could see nobody in the room.

They glanced around searching for a ghost but there was none to be seen. The top floor was almost bare except for a giant lighting apparatus in the center of the room.

Looking around, Jonah saw the culprit. There was an open window at the far end of the room, on the other side of the lighting apparatus. He scoffed to himself. Annie was right this whole time, and here they were freaking out and trying to escape over an open window.

He strode across the room to close the window.

Jonah grabbed the window and paused for a moment to admire the view before shutting and latching it.

That's when he saw it.

In the reflection of the window, he could make out a figure looming behind him.

Chapter Eleven

Jonah swung around to see a man getting to his feet. The first thing he noticed was how tall the man was. His clothes were stained with grease and grime, and the man was slowly chewing on a toothpick. Though they had just barged into the room, he didn't look too surprised to see them.

"W-who are you?" Jonah stammered to the man.

The man pulled a filthy rag out of his back pocket and began cleaning off a wrench in his hand that Jonah hadn't noticed earlier. He glanced down the bridge of his nose at each member of the group before responding.

"My name is Henry Whitaker. I am the caretaker for this island," the man said.

Jonah was stunned. He had seen the state of the buildings on the island, and if there was a caretaker then he was doing a horrendous job. Though he wasn't going to mention it to the man currently towering over him while holding a wrench.

"It's not often that people come out here," Henry said. He continued to wipe down his wrench, though with the state of that rag, there was no way it would be coming along cleaner than before. "Not

Welcome To Nightmare Island

the smartest idea to be poking around on an island filled with ghosts, but I'm not here to guide all your decisions. Maverick didn't tell me there were going to be visitors, he tends to try to keep people away."

Seeing that the caretaker seemed to wish them no harm, Jonah called the girls up from the first floor. They were startled upon first seeing Henry, who introduced himself to the newcomers with a smile.

"I'm sorry to barge in on you like this," Jonah said. "We were exploring the island when we stumbled upon the lighthouse, and we couldn't resist coming in. We had some free time before the next part of the tour started and we felt like it wouldn't hurt to explore as long as we had these on." With that, he held up his wrist, showing the bracelet pulsing with blue light.

"Maverick is giving tours now? That's news to me. But what do I know, I'm just the caretaker." He wiped down his wrench once more, reminding Jonah of a bartender cleaning a glass. "Well, it's hard not to flock to the one thing of beauty in a world filled with ugly," Henry said. "I've been up here for a few hours now. Been tinkering with the mechanisms in this light to see if I can get it working again. There are so many things on this island that have gone to shit over the years, and there ain't enough time in the day to fix them all."

"I was gonna say," Kevin chimed in. "Some of these buildings are looking pretty rough."

Annie glared at Kevin.

Kevin continued, "Last night I was trying to get to sleep, and the faucet in my bathroom just kept on dripping no matter how tight I turned the handle. Do you mind fixing it when you get the chance?"

Henry glared at Kevin. "I'll add it to my list," he said sarcastically. "Mainly my job is to make sure that the signal tower is up to par. If that thing goes down, then we will be the next ghosts to be stranded on this island."

He pointed through the window behind them. Jonah turned, seeing the signal tower off in the distance, its light pulsing steadily.

Just then, they heard a low rumble in the distance. Henry turned to see rolling black clouds coming in from across the lake. His face turned distraught.

"It wasn't supposed to storm today," Henry said biting his lip. "You ought to get back to your rooms. There are many ways to die on this island even without the ghosts."

"Sorry to bother you, we'll be on our way," Jonah said. Beginning to move toward the stairs, he turned around and said "Is there another exit in this place? We only came up here because we couldn't get the door open."

Henry grinned. "Those doors are meant to withstand thirty-foot waves. They won't open by simply pulling on the handle. There's a trick to getting them open." He followed the group down the stairs. Reaching the door, he simply grabbed the handle and lifted slightly. To Chuck and Kevin's dismay, the door opened easily for the man.

"Get on now," Henry continued.

Chuck and the others walked through the door, with Kevin taking up the lead. Just then, Jonah felt a hand grip his shoulder. He turned to see Henry, whose face had grown serious once more.

"I wouldn't spend too much time on this island if I were you. The moment that boat comes, you get off this little piece of hell, you understand me?" Henry said.

Jonah gulped, looking down at Henry's hand on his shoulder. He was old, but his grip was something fierce.

"Yes sir," Jonah said.

Henry let go of his shoulder, and Jonah began to walk through the door after his friends. He thought of something else he wanted to ask Henry, but when he turned around, the man was gone.

Chapter Twelve

Miles led the group of friends to a remote part of the island for the second night of their tour. This location was far from any of the ones they had gone to the night before, and the fog wasn't as strong on this side of the island.

This made it very easy for them to see the building that rose before them.

"Welcome to Graystone Manor," Miles said, making a sweeping gesture with his arms.

The group stood in awe of the building in front of them. It stood out wildly from the rest of the buildings they had seen on the island. Graystone Manor was a Victorian-era mansion on the edge of the island, with views of the lake stretching behind it. Though it looked older than any building they had seen, it was also the most beautiful. With a huge porch and giant windows, the home was something that one could wish to retire to, to spend countless evenings watching the sunset over the lake whilst sitting on a rocking chair on the porch.

That would be if it wasn't on this island. Also, it seemed in vast need of repair.

The paint on the siding was crumbling away, and many pieces of the siding were lopsided or had fallen off altogether. The glass of every window except one seemed to be blown out. The porch railing was missing a few rungs, and the roof featured several holes the size of a highland cow.

They each stood there, mouths agape, taking in the scenery and imagining how this property must have looked new.

"Graystone Manor used to belong to the owners of the island. The *first* owners of the island," Miles clarified. "The Graystone family were very wealthy, and they had decided to buy the island and build a house on it several hundred years ago. From what I'm told, they were a very happy family. The owner had grown rich from the oil trade and wanted to give his family a private destination with 360-degree lake views. His wife would stay home and clean the house, and cook supper for the kids, who spent their days playing on the island." With this, Miles gestured toward where they had come from.

"The family was very happy living on the island, at first. But alas, that's where the first atrocity on the island can be attributed." Miles said.

"What happened?" Annie asked.

"Did the rich guy get bored one day and kill his wife?" Kevin asked.

"Shut up," Chuck said, smacking him on the shoulder.

"No," Miles said with a disapproving look on his face. "One day, while her husband was away, the mistress of the house told the kids to go outside and play. After a few minutes, she began to call them back inside, one by one. First came the daughter. The mistress shut the curtains, took out a razor blade, and slit her daughter's throat from ear to ear. The boys heard a commotion and ran inside, only to be met with a similar fate soon thereafter."

"Oh my god," Audrey choked out, covering her mouth with her hand. "That's horrible."

Miles continued, "Mr. Graystone came home that night to a ghastly sight. He opened the door and found a trail of bodies leading into the bedroom. These were the bodies of his only daughter, his oldest son, and finally, his youngest son, who was just a toddler at the time. He followed the bodies into the bedroom where he found the body of his wife."

Jonah looked up at the beautiful house, trying to picture the events of that night, while at the same time trying to hide the thought of them from his memory.

"The wife was the worst of them all. After taking the lives of her three children, she turned the razor blade on herself. After slitting her own throat, she felt that she wasn't dying fast enough. So, she went back with the blade again and again, attacking her own throat with so much force that when her husband finally found her, the razor blade was still stuck inside her neck."

With this, Annie wiped a tear away from her face. She had grown up in a household with several siblings and couldn't imagine something like this happening to them.

"Mr. Graystone was overcome with emotion. He was the only one left of his family. The only person left on the island. There was nobody to express his grief to. And nobody to stop him from taking his own life. He pointed a shotgun at his head and pulled the trigger. And that was the end of the Graystone family's tenure on this island, and on this earth. Though some have said that they could still see Mrs. Graystone standing at the window of the third floor, beckoning to each of her children to come in and meet their fates."

Jonah looked up at the third floor. There stood the only window that still held its glass. He could imagine someone standing behind the pane of glass, beckoning for him to come in. It reminded him of the thing he thought he saw at the fourth-floor window of the hotel.

Jonah shivered. It was just a trick of the fog, he reminded himself.

Chapter Thirteen

Miles led them up the stairs of Graystone Manor, tapping each step to test for rot before placing his full weight on it. Each of them followed behind, not so eager to meet whatever the island had tucked away in this house of horrors.

Jonah was the last to reach the top of the porch. He looked around at the paint peeling off the walls, the holes in the deck, and the railing that had collapsed under its own weight. He didn't know how safe he felt being on this porch. Looking up, he saw a rocking chair in the corner swaying in the wind.

Except, there wasn't any wind to be felt.

As Miles led the friends inside, they were surprised by how much the house had retained from the Graystone days. It was like walking into a time capsule.

The children's shoes still lay near the front door, caked in mud from rainy days of centuries past. Their coats still hung on the coat rack in the corner, never to be used again.

On the mantle, there stood a massive family portrait, a thick layer of glass preserving it after all this time. It displayed the young girl and her brother, along with the toddler cradled in his mother's arms. Mr.

Welcome To Nightmare Island

Graystone looked on stout and proud at the camera. Mrs. Graystone looked just like any other normal person. There didn't seem to be anything off about her. She didn't look like the kind of person who would randomly kill her three children and then take her own life.

Jonah stared at the photo, wondering what could have driven the woman to commit such a terrible act against the members of her own household.

As they strolled through the house, they noticed other things left over from the past. There were dishes still in the sink, as well as a bowl full of fruit on the table that had long since turned black with rot. Around the bowl of fruit, the table was still set for a supper that would never come.

They were taken up the stairs, noticing a distinct change from the downstairs. This floor was much closer to the holes in the roof and had therefore experienced much more weather damage than the downstairs had. The wallpaper had begun peeling off in full sheets, and many pieces had been ripped to shreds, presumably by birds trying to use it as material for nests. The floorboards had been warped from water damage and many areas were covered in a layer of black mold.

The group turned down the hall, where they were met with a grisly sight.

The wood floors were still stained from the blood of the slaughtered children. They could still see where each body had fallen, preserved over hundreds of years. Something like that would never scrub clean. The memories of such a traumatic event itself would haunt these halls forever.

Annie gulped, pointing her flashlight down the hall, following the blood trail to a closed door.

"Is that where we're going?" Annie asked.

Miles said nothing but led them toward the door all the same. He reached for the handle, testing the cold steel in his hands, before revealing its contents to them.

Chapter Fourteen

The door swung open with a loud creak.
Jonah braced for the worst, and he got it.
The blood trail continued into this room, and it led to the edge of the bed, which was coated in dried blood. The blood stains spread out under the bed until they were swallowed up by darkness.

Jonah remembered the story that Miles had told them. Mrs. Graystone must have slit her own throat at the edge of the bed. The marks on the floor were all that were left of her. Then he remembered that the husband had come home.

He brought his flashlight around the room until he saw what he was looking for, and it was a memory he wouldn't soon forget.

On the wall opposite the bed, there was a massive blood splatter leading up to the ceiling. Jonah's light followed the mess upwards, where he found a hole in the roof. Part of Mr. Graystone's shotgun blast must have killed him, while the rest of the shot must have blown a hole in the ceiling.

Jonah brought the beam of his light back down, and what he saw made him freeze in his tracks.

Welcome To Nightmare Island

The rest of the group jumped in alarm when they saw the man on the floor.

They had grown so accustomed to the thought that there may not be a ghost here that it had genuinely taken them aback to see anything at all.

The man on the ground was bald, with dark tattoos covering most of the visible skin on his head. He was sitting cross-legged on the ground as if he was meditating.

Jonah wondered if the man was a monk, but then dismissed the thought immediately. No religious being would ever step foot in this hell hole.

Only then did he notice the blue veil at the edge of the room. They had been so focused on the remnants of the Graystone family that they hadn't noticed the field of energy that tended to separate them from the malicious spirits on this island.

"This is Javier," Miles said.

The man on the ground seemed to twitch as his name was spoken aloud.

"When Maverick caught up to him," Miles went on, "Javier had decided to take a stroll through a suburban neighborhood. In every house that he walked by, one of the residents inside would go into a fit of uncontrollable rage. They would then murder every person in the residence before ending their own lives."

They all looked at the man on the floor. He seemed to be focusing his thoughts elsewhere. He was staring at the ground as if he wasn't interested in the other occupants of the room.

"Javier has the power to alter your mind, to fill it with homicidal thoughts. When he gets into your head, the only thing that feels like it will end the torture inside your brain is murder.

He will turn his attention on one person in a group and use that person to kill everyone around him."

The man on the ground slowly twisted his neck to the side, stopping only once an audible crack echoed around the room.

Miles stopped to look back at the man on the floor, before returning to what he was saying.

"Javier enjoys listening to the screams of the dying. He likes to hear the confusion in the voices of his victims as they are hacked to death by someone they thought was their friend or family."

They turned their attention back to Javier, whose head was hung low. Slowly, he lifted his eyes to meet theirs.

Jonah cringed at the sight. Javier's eyes weren't like those of a normal person. The bags under them were dark purple. The whites of his eyes were a deep crimson, and his pupils were of the darkest black that Jonah had ever seen.

Jonah's blood ran cold. He felt like he could feel Javier's eyes piercing his soul. Jonah quickly looked back at Miles, avoiding the gaze of Javier.

"Maverick had tracked down Javier in Columbia, where he had been known to ignite violence in the streets. Javier had used his powers to start gang wars and had caused the senseless deaths of numerous innocent women and children," Miles said.

With that, a twinge of a smile graced the face of the ghost, who obviously took great glee in the idea of the death of those unable to protect themselves.

"Though he has never physically touched any of his victims, Javier is responsible for more deaths than any other ghost on this island," Miles said.

Jonah looked back at the spot where Javier was sitting on the ground, except he wasn't there. Looking around, he spotted him, now standing a hairs breadth behind Miles. The only thing standing between him, and their tour guide was the force field which slowly pulsed its blue glow throughout the room.

Javier traced his fingers along the wall of light, testing the boundary that kept him from ending the lives of everyone in the room. The wall hummed as he touched it as if reinforcing its intent to keep him out.

Welcome To Nightmare Island

The hum got Miles's attention, and he spun around, startled at how close the ghost had gotten to him without him knowing.

Javier never took his wicked eyes off the tour guide. It was as if he was figuring out which member of the group had the weakest mind or was more likely to turn on the other members. It reminded Jonah of a lion tracking down the oldest and unhealthiest gazelle in the pack to take for its next meal.

Miles took a moment to compose himself, taking a handkerchief out of his pocket to clear his throat. Then he went on. "One of the worst parts about Javier is that you'll never hear him coming. As I'm sure you've noticed, he doesn't have the same characteristics of the other ghosts. He doesn't have a foul smell or heavy breathing. You don't hear him eating people like you might with the rest. In fact, if you ever see him outside of these force fields, it's probably already too late."

Miles looked down at his watch. "We need to move on to the next room."

The group followed him out. Jonah could feel the eyes of Javier watching them as he left. He had a feeling it wouldn't be the last time he felt those eyes on him.

Chapter Fifteen

The group walked slowly toward their next destination. The fog around them had grown so thick that they had trouble seeing the person next to them.

"Ow!" Chuck said holding his shin. He had just tripped over a large object sticking out of the ground. Was it a rock? A stump? He shone his flashlight on the object, and the group came to a halt.

"Are we walking through a cemetery?" Annie asked, looking down at the tombstone that Chuck had just tripped on. Her voice was shrill as she questioned Miles. Ghosts were okay in her book, but cemeteries were where she drew the line. Every one of her friends knew of her fear of cemeteries, but she had never told them why.

Jonah pondered this for a while. It could be the fear of the dead rising that scared her or the fear of falling into an open grave and being buried alive. Or maybe it was the thought of what happens when you were buried that freaks her out. The image of the worms squirming in through a gap in the coffin door, of the maggots slowly crawling across your skin as they nibbled on your skin, laying eggs in your decaying flesh, and making a home out of your rotting corpse.

Welcome To Nightmare Island

Jonah shuddered. The more he thought about it, the more he tended to agree with Annie's fear of cemeteries.

He swung his flashlight around, taking in the stones around them, each depicting the birth and death dates of those who have deceased.

"Yes, we are walking through a cemetery," Miles said. "These are where all the bodies of those who have died on this island are buried. Nobody who has died on this island has ever left. Those who live off the island believed that the bodies of those who died here would be cursed to walk the earth forever, and they refused to accept the bodies of their deceased loved ones." He swung his flashlight around at the gravestones. "The survivors on the island were forced to bury their friends here, to prevent the curse from spreading outside the island."

As the group looked around them, they became lost in just how many gravestones littered the grounds. There must have been hundreds of them. How many people had died on this island?

"We mustn't stay too long, we have to get on with the rest of the tour," Miles said.

The look of relief on Annie's face was tremendous. For a second there, she had thought that the next ghost would be stationed in the cemetery, and she didn't know if she could handle that.

"The next location is down this way," Miles said, pointing his flashlight past some gravestones. His light was stopped short by the fog, and the group was unable to see what he was pointing at.

Annie didn't seem to care what was ahead. The less time she could spend in this cemetery, the better. She walked ahead toward the way Miles had shown, eager to leave this area. It was a few moments before she realized that she had no idea where she was going, and she turned back to let Miles take the lead again.

Miles led the group through headstone after headstone, some covered by bushes and moss.

This cemetery was severely unkempt, and Jonah thought that Henry had his work cut out for him.

As they went, the headstones grew older and older, eventually fading until they could no longer read the epitaph etched into the stones.

Finally, Miles brought them up to a rickety iron fence. It was the kind of fence that normally enclosed a plot given to a family who could afford to have their own section of the graveyard. The tall iron fence was topped with ornate spikes as if to keep people out of the area.

Or to keep something in.

Miles led them to a gate on the side of the fence. The gate was covered in rusty chains, topped off with the largest padlock Jonah had ever seen.

Reaching into his pocket, Miles pulled out a loop of keys. Finding the one he wanted, he grabbed the padlock on the gate and inserted the key. With a satisfying click, the lock popped open. Miles began the long process of unraveling the rusty chains, turning his hands orange in doing so. Whatever was in there, they really didn't want it to come out.

Finally, Miles dropped the chain on the ground and pushed on the gate. Except, it didn't budge.

The earth around the gate had grown dense with foliage. From how tall the weeds were in front of the gate, Jonah guessed that nobody had been out here in years.

Annie seemed happy that the gate wasn't working, but her frown returned as Miles put the weight of his body into pushing the door open.

With a rusty squeal, the door swung open, kicking up a mountain of dirt in the process.

Taking a few deep breaths, Miles picked up his flashlight and pointed it onward. Apparently, they hadn't reached their destination yet.

After a few paces, they came upon what appeared to be a bunker built into the side of a hill. A concrete wall curved in, leading to a door in the center of the wall.

Welcome To Nightmare Island

"Welcome to the crypt of the Black Witch," Miles said swinging his arms toward the door.

Annie seemed ready to burst. Her face had gone sheer white, and her breathing was heavy. She looked like she might be having a panic attack.

"Crypt? I can't go into a crypt," Annie said.

Miles turned to look at her. "Well, why not? Afraid you might see a ghost?" Miles asked with a smirk.

Annie didn't answer, but they could see the reluctance on her face.

"Nobody is going to force you to go into the crypt," Miles said. "But if you choose not to do so, you will have to cut your tour early and walk back to the hotel. Alone."

Annie gulped, looking back at the cemetery behind her. "Alone?"

"Yes, alone," Miles said. "I must be here to lead the tour, and there is nobody else on the island who can walk you back. And I cannot guarantee your safety on the way back." Miles swung back toward the mausoleum. "Do what you must," he said uncaringly.

Annie spun around, looking back at where they came from. Then, taking a deep breath, she steeled herself full of courage and turned back toward the crypt. "I'll stay," Annie said.

"Thought you would," Miles said. It was clear in his tone of voice that he didn't give a damn what her decision was gonna be. "Since you're staying, why don't you be a dear and get the door for us."

"Me? G-get the door?" Annie said shakily.

"Yes," Miles said rolling his eyes. "Who else have I been talking to for the last few minutes?"

Annie gulped, taking a few steps forward. The door was old and made of heavy oak wood. There was a glass viewing window on the front, with bars going across it. As Annie walked closer, she could feel her chest tighten as her fear of what lay beyond that door grew. She realized she was holding her breath, and she let it out with a whoosh. It instantly turned to mist in front of her, and through that mist, she thought she could see a face in the window.

She gasped, turning back to face Miles.

"There's somebody there!" Annie shouted at him.

"Where?" Miles asked.

Annie turned back toward the door, but there was nobody there. It must have been a trick of the mist. Steadying herself, she reached for the door handle. The metal was cold in her hands.

Like everything in this part of the cemetery, the door was ancient, and it stuck when she pulled it.

She was growing frustrated trying to get it open. The faster they got through this, the faster they could get the hell out of this cemetery.

Using two hands, she got a firm grip on the door handle and pulled with all her might.

It opened with a grinding noise. The weather-beaten door had sagged on its hinges over time and the bottom of the wood ground against the concrete below as it opened.

Annie fell back, expecting the specter she had seen behind the glass to be standing on the other side. But once more, there was nothing there, or at least, nothing that she could see. The doorway was pitch black, hiding all the contents inside.

Annie sat back, panting as Miles walked past her.

"Watch your step," Miles said. Then he disappeared into the crypt.

Chapter Sixteen

Jonah didn't like the way that Miles was treating Annie. None of them did. In fact, they were all beginning to really dislike Miles.

Was his attitude toward them all an act? Just a part of the tour? They couldn't tell.

But sticking up for Annie could put one of them in the hot seat.

Annie wasn't the only one who didn't want to walk into the crypt. That thing was downright creepy.

They could all feel something. Something like a presence lurking right inside that doorway, while also simultaneously all around them, pushing them toward its cavernous dark mouth.

None of them wanted to go inside, but at least inside the crypt, there was one man who knew what he was doing. If anything went wrong, he would know how to handle it, right?

Jonah looked around at his surroundings. The mist seemed to be closing in on them, gently corralling them all toward the crypt.

He shivered. Then walked through the entrance and into the darkness.

Nothing could have prepared him for what came next. It felt like stepping out of the comfort of your warm harm into the eye of the storm. So many emotions and feelings hit him at once.

Jonah was struck by a sudden sense of claustrophobia as he descended the steps. His nose felt clogged with the scent of wet earth and decay. It smelled like they were storing dead bodies in this space, which he realized with sudden dismay, they were.

He jumped as he felt a hand on his shoulder.

Looking back, he saw that the rest of the group had fallen in behind him.

Jonah took a deep breath, his courage slightly mustered again. He pushed on, down a few more steps.

He was just thinking about the fact that he hadn't seen Miles yet when he heard a sound that made his blood run cold.

From the depths of the crypt came a blood-curdling scream. It reverberated against the walls of the stairwell that he and his friends were on, and it made his heart stop beating for a few seconds.

Jonah forgot how to breathe.

He and his friends stood stock still on the stairs, listening intently for any other sounds.

Then it came again. A wretched wail pierced their eardrums.

What was down there? Who was screaming? What could possibly possess someone to make a sound so foul, so sorrowful, so full of pain and anguish?

Jonah had to find out. Slowly he began to descend the last of the steps. Flashlight in front of him, he led the way, taking each step carefully, listening for anything that might be headed in their direction.

Reaching the bottom step, he lifted his flashlight and nearly jumped out of his skin.

Miles was standing an inch in front of him, shielding his face from the light.

"Can you point that thing somewhere else?" Miles asked.

"Sorry," Jonah said pointing the light back at the ground.

"What took you so long?" Miles asked as the rest of the group descended the stairs.

Welcome To Nightmare Island

Annie glared at him with daggers in her eyes.

Miles just smiled and said, "We're headed this way."

He pointed toward a passage behind him, where a faint blue glow could be seen shimmering against the walls.

They all knew what that meant. There was a ghost nearby.

"What was all that screaming we heard?" Kevin asked. He had halted where he stood and didn't seem to want to move until he had an answer.

"You're about to find out," Miles said.

Chapter Seventeen

Walking through the passage, Jonah touched his glowing wristband anxiously. If there was anything down here that would attack them, he hoped this metal band would do what their tour guide said it would. He didn't quite believe that it would help, but to be fair, yesterday he hadn't really believed ghosts were real either.

He walked into the room and stood there bewildered. He had never been inside a crypt before, so he didn't know what to expect.

There were torches along the walls, their flames casting shadows across the room. Caskets filled cubbies lined every inch of the walls. Cobwebs seemed to cover everything in sight. But what really stood out in the room was the casket in the center of the room.

It stood on a platform raised in the center of the room, with a stairway of bones leading up to it.

Jonah looked around the room, expecting to see something, or rather someone, who had made those wretched screams. Through the torchlight, he thought he could make out figures all around them, but it was just the light from the torches making shadows dance around the room. He didn't know what could be lurking in those shadows, ready to pounce at them the moment they turned their backs.

Just to be sure, he took a step back, making sure he was completely clear of the barrier that was supposed to keep them safe.

"Where did those screams come from?" Kevin asked. His normally joking demeanor was gone, and he grit his teeth in anticipation of the answer. He had the feeling that he didn't want to know, but his curiosity got the better of him.

Miles turned to look at them.

"This crypt belongs to the Black Witch," Miles said with a smile. "Those screams you heard came from inside the stone casket."

With that, Miles pointed at the casket in the center of the room.

"The Black Witch's spirit is thousands of years old. Maverick believed that her power may be too strong even to be contained in the barrier, so he trapped her far underground, far from anything else on the island. He placed her inside a stone casket and then chained the casket closed. The lid on that thing alone probably weighs over 3000 pounds."

Another wretched scream came from inside the casket. Jonah felt like it went on forever.

Annie closed her eyes, taking a step back toward the door. Her fists were clenched so hard that her fingernails bit into the palms of her hand, bringing the slightest hint of blood to the surface.

Kevin pressed his hands to his ears. The screams were so loud that they bounced all over the room, making it seem like they were coming from in front of him, as well as from behind him.

Suddenly, the casket began to shake, rattling the chains around it. The lid of the casket was bouncing up and down against the restraints. Dust clouds blew out from the seams of the casket, where stone had rubbed against stone, grinding the edges of her cell into dust.

Miles's face went white, staring at the Black Witch's tomb until it finally went silent. Gaining his composure once more, Miles continued.

"As you can see, the Black Witch is very powerful, and she does not like being chained up. Unfortunately, we will not be able to see her today, as doing so would result in the untimely deaths of everyone in this room." Miles said. His normal arrogant attitude seemed to have faded away, scared out of him by the tantrum of the Black Witch.

"What happens if she gets out of the casket?" Jonah asked.

Annie squirmed where she stood. She didn't want to think of the possibility of that happening.

Miles shifted on his feet nervously. Apparently, he didn't feel too comfortable with the idea either. "Should the Black Witch escape her tomb, and get through the barrier, Maverick had installed a fail-safe. There is a sensor on the stairs that detects paranormal activity. Should the sensors read a powerful enough paranormal presence on the stairs, the sensor would trip a fuse, causing the whole crypt to cave in, trapping the Black Witch inside."

Annie bit her lip. She didn't like the idea of being inside a place where there was a chance that she might be buried alive.

"Shall we move on to the next ghost?" Miles asked, waving toward the stairs.

He didn't have to ask them twice. Annie was already bounding up the stairs two at a time.

Chapter Eighteen

For the next location, Miles led the group into a building that they weren't quite expecting to see on this trip. It seemed almost...normal?

They walked through the halls and were greeted not by trails of blood or the smell of death, but instead by the smell of books.

Miles had led them into a library.

Jonah looked around, wondering what they were doing in such a place. After all the things that they had seen, there was no way that this was the end of the tour. It was too peaceful. Too reminiscent of home.

As he looked around at the dust-coated bookshelves around him, Jonah could almost picture one of his own books adorning these very shelves.

"What are we doing here?" Chuck asked.

"I'm leading you to the last ghost of the tour," Miles said.

"But in a library?" Kevin exclaimed. "Don't you have some creepy dungeon to lead us down to or something? I mean, not that I'm complaining, but it seems a bit out of character with the rest of the tour."

"I wasn't in charge of assigning the rooms for the ghosts," Miles said. "But on the way out I will gladly lock you in a damp cell if that is what you would prefer." With this, he smiled at Kevin, half hoping that the idiot would give him permission to do just that.

"Nah, I think I'm gonna pass on that one," Kevin said, stepping away from Miles.

They walked past a few more shelves before coming upon the familiar pulsing blue light.

The group was in a dark corner of the library, lit mostly by the light rebounding off the barrier wall. The tomes on the shelves were thick and leatherbound and seemed to be hundreds of years old, much like everything else on the island.

But they still didn't see a ghost, or smell one for that matter.

"Hmm, she may have her nose pressed into a book," Miles said looking around.

That was the last thing Jonah was expecting to hear about a ghost. Normally, when he thought of ghosts, he didn't think of them perusing the fiction section of the local library.

"Oh, Mabel!" Miles called out.

Suddenly, Mabel walked into view from behind one of the bookcases.

The jaws of every person in the room dropped.

Mabel was stunning.

Beyond prettier than any living person that Jonah had ever seen, his girlfriend included, Mabel waltzed across the library floor with grace. She paused a few steps in front of the barrier, examining the latest visitors to her library.

Mabel was very attractive, though dressed like she was from the Victorian era. She had full pouty lips and eyelashes that fluttered whenever she looked at them. They did nothing to hide her bright blue eyes, which now were staring deep into Jonah's.

"Ahem," Audrey coughed, bringing them all back into the moment.

"Meet Mabel," Miles said, smiling at the ghost.

Welcome To Nightmare Island

At this, Mabel reached her hand out as if to shake hands, but her fingers touched the barrier, shocking her and making her take a step back. There she stood, rubbing her hand, and glancing up at Miles with a pouting look on her face.

"I know, I know. How could they lock you up in a place like this?" Miles said sarcastically to the ghost. "Don't let Mabel's looks deceive you. She may be astonishingly pretty…"

With this, Mabel blushed at Miles.

"But she also has the power to alter your perception of reality. She was known to lure in unsuspecting men with her looks, then as soon as they got close, she would send their minds on a trip somewhere far away. One minute a man would be walking down a dark alley toward a pretty girl, and the next moment he thinks he's in Hawaii, growing old on a beach somewhere surrounded by girls in bikinis. If he's lucky."

He smiled at the pretty ghost on the other side of the barrier and continued. "Unfortunately, you don't get to decide what visions you see. Only she can choose that for you. If you piss her off, you may open your eyes and find that you're in a fiery pit in hell, with both arms amputated and your mouth sewn shut. I don't recommend getting on this one's bad side."

"Mabel doesn't seem too dangerous," Annie said. "Why is she locked up on this island?"

"She may not be the most murderous ghost on the island, but she has caused a lot of trouble over the past few hundred years. There would be reports of a pretty girl in a white dress along the side of the road hitchhiking. At one point, you're driving on the highway, and the next moment Mabel has altered your mind to think you're somewhere else. Yet you and your vehicle are still careening at high speeds into oncoming traffic, killing innocent people."

Jonah looked at Mabel. It was hard to picture her causing the deaths of countless people for hundreds of years.

Miles went on, "It was even worse when people who ran into her survived. The tales that went around of a drop-dead gorgeous girl wandering around with the power to instantly transport your mind to paradise, led many men to try to find her. Though many that did end up going crazy after being exposed to her mind-altering powers. Ever wonder why there were so many insane asylums back in the day? You can thank Mabel for increasing their popularity."

Miles stole a look at his watch. "It's about time your tour comes to an end. Say goodbye to Mabel and we will be on our way."

Jonah reached into his pocket, pulling out his father's pocket watch to check the time.

Miles glanced down at Jonah's pocket watch, his eyes widening as he noticed the symbol that adorned the casing.

Jonah snapped the lid of the watch closed. He looked back up at Miles, who had adjusted his face before anyone had seen the look of excitement in his eyes.

"Shall we?" Miles asked, pointing toward the exit.

Chapter Nineteen

"That's an interesting watch you have there," Miles said to Jonah on the walk back to the hotel. "Most people these days rely on their phones to check the time."

"I probably would too," Jonah said. "Except with there being no service on the island, I thought I would leave my phone in the hotel to conserve the battery for the ride home. And I never go anywhere without my pocket watch. It was a gift from my father, and it had been passed down from generation to generation for hundreds of years. Apparently, as the story goes, one of my long-deceased great-grandfathers fancied himself to be a ghosthunter like Maverick. The love of chasing ghosts and ghost stories was passed down to each generation along with this watch."

"Hmm." Miles seemed lost in his own thoughts as they traveled through the fog. He looked to the sky as a rumble echoed around them. There was a storm coming their way.

Jonah rubbed his thumb against the cold metal lid of the pocket watch. Nobody had taken an interest in it before other than him or the other members of his family. Normally when he pulled it out to check the time, his friends would make fun of him for carrying the relic around.

"Why do you still have that piece of junk?" Kevin would ask. "You're a successful author now, it's about time you throw out that tetanus shot waiting to happen and buy yourself a nice Rolex. And while you're at it, if you're feeling generous, my wrists could use some bling too."

Jonah would always dismiss his friends' efforts to get him to ditch the pocket watch. It was a family heirloom. And it had been passed down for hundreds of years for a reason, he just didn't know what reason yet.

A lightning strike illuminated the outline of the hotel, only a few hundred yards in front of them. The group sped up a bit, eager to get out of the rain and put some distance between them and the ghosts.

Suddenly, someone bumped into Jonah from behind, sending him crashing to the ground.

"Ow, watch where you're walking!" Jonah said. He pulled some loose gravel bits from his palms, then looked up, surprised to see Miles standing there with his hand out. He grabbed it, pulling himself to a standing position.

"Try not to get yourselves hurt before the boat comes to get you tomorrow. I'm sure none of you would like to pay another visit to the infirmary." Miles grinned at his own joke. "The boat will be back at the dock at sunrise. If you miss the boat, you may be stuck here for quite some time. Try to get some rest."

With that, he left the group at the doors to the hotel and walked off into the storm. After a few seconds, he disappeared entirely.

The group staggered toward the elevator, shaking raindrops off their clothes as they walked. The lights flickered as the storm raged outside, but none of them seemed to notice. Their minds were still on the sights they had seen that night. The horrors of Nightmare Island kept running through their minds. They were so distracted by the memories of the night that they paid no mind to the elevator as it dinged.

Welcome To Nightmare Island

The doors opened with the usual clanging, and they all stepped inside.

Had they all forgotten what had happened in the elevator only twenty-four hours ago? Of course not, but their minds were on the freshest dose of harsh reality that the island had given them tonight.

As the elevator doors closed, none of them said a word. They each just stared blankly into the distance. They would have continued this way if it weren't for the storm.

A sudden thunderclap rang out overhead. It was so loud and so close that it seemed to shake the very foundation of the building. They all ducked as if expecting the roof to come down upon them. It didn't.

But something much worse happened.

The power went out. The elevator came to a shrieking halt. The lights shut off, plunging them into complete darkness.

Annie began to freak out. She didn't like elevators to begin with, and she had known from the first time she saw it that this elevator in particular was bad news. Now they were trapped in a rickety metal box several stories up in complete darkness.

What was going to happen to them? This thing had been installed way before emergency backup lights had been invented.

"Does this elevator have an emergency call button?" Audrey asked.

"For what?" Kevin asked. "Who is going to come? You think emergency crews are going to drive out in this storm all the way to the lake, then commandeer a rowboat and come save us in the middle of the night from a hotel that shouldn't have occupants?"

Jonah frowned to himself. He had to admit, their options seemed bleak.

The friends stood there in silence, listening to the sounds of the storm outside. The walls were thin, so they could hear everything. They heard rain slapping the windowsills. They could hear the mice scratching at the walls somewhere nearby. Thunder drummed off in the distance.

Devin Cabrera

Now that the elevator had stopped, they noticed that it had some sway to it. Jonah could only imagine the dark chasm they were hanging over. One false move and they could all go plunging to their deaths.

Everyone in the elevator seemed to be thinking the same thing, trying not to breathe for the fear of making the elevator shift at all.

Then all at once, the lights flickered back on.

They all looked at each other, finally permitting themselves to take a deep breath. Jonah smiled at Audrey. They were going to be okay; they would laugh about this in the future. They just had to get off this godforsaken island. Tomorrow morning couldn't come soon enough.

They could hear the elevator motors in the shaft below them begin to boot back up again.

Then suddenly, it shuddered to life. The elevator was climbing higher and higher. The group couldn't be more relieved to be moving again. That is until it went past the third floor once more.

Jonah looked at the panel of buttons. The third-floor button was no longer lit up. When they had lost power, the elevator must have reset itself. It probably had a startup sequence where it would cycle through each floor as a test protocol to make sure everything was working again.

And it was starting on the fourth floor.

The rest of the group seemed to come to this same realization. Chuck began slamming his finger against the third-floor button, willing it to change directions, but to no avail. The elevator seemed to have its course mapped out, and it wasn't going to budge from that.

They watched in terror as the elevator came to a stop. Jonah became briefly aware that he was holding his breath.

They stared at the doors, not wishing to see what monstrosity was on the other side. After what seemed like an eternity, the elevator dinged, and the doors slid open.

The group stood there with bated breath. The whole floor was dark except for the faint glow that came from the open elevator doors.

Welcome To Nightmare Island

Jonah squinted his eyes, trying to get them to adjust to the darkness. But he couldn't see anything.

Jonah leaned forward, pressing the button to close the doors. After a brief pause, the doors began to close once more.

With a brief flash and a loud rumble of thunder from outside, the lights flickered and went out again. The door remained half open, the lack of power preventing it from closing fully.

The group waited in silence, but when the power didn't come back on, Jonah knew they had to do something.

He turned to face his group of friends, or where he thought they were standing. It was hard to be sure because it was pitch black in the room. "It doesn't seem like the power is coming back on," Jonah said. "Either we stay here and wait for the power to come back on, or we go and see if we can find a stairwell we can use."

"Are you crazy?" Annie said in a hushed voice. "You were on the elevator with us when we saw that thing. There is something on this floor, and if we go out there, we could die."

"Does anyone have any better alternatives?" Jonah asked the room. "Because if we don't find another way out, then we are stuck in a room with nowhere to go. And then if whatever is up here decides to check out the elevator, we're as good as dead. So, until the power comes back on, our best bet is to try to find another way off this floor before that thing finds us."

Audrey glared silently at Jonah. He couldn't see her face, but from her silence he could tell that she didn't approve of this venture. He wasn't so sure of it himself, but in the end, it was their only hope.

"I'm going out there to look for another exit. The rest of you can stay here. I'll go and report back with what I find," Jonah said.

"You're not going out there by yourself," Audrey said in a hushed whisper.

"Well, I'm not taking you out there with me. It could be dangerous, and the safest place to be is on the elevator. If the power comes on, you can take the elevator to safety," Jonah said.

"I'm coming with you," Chuck said. He stepped out of the elevator to join Jonah.

"Okay," Jonah said taking a deep breath. "We'll look for an exit and be back as soon as we can. If that thing comes back, make yourself unseen and don't make a sound."

With that, he and Chuck began to tiptoe down the hallway.

They walked carefully, one step at a time. Jonah put one foot in front as the other, testing to make sure that the floor wouldn't give out below him. They listened carefully to hear if the thing was nearby, but all they could hear was the patter of rain against the windows and the rumble of thunder in the distance.

A flash of lightning briefly lit up the hall in front of them, and they could make out several doorways to either side of them. The doorframes were covered in plastic sheeting, which swayed in an unseen draft. There must be an open window or a hole in the roof somewhere, Jonah thought.

Jonah stopped near one of the doorways, lightly pulling the plastic sheeting to one side to see the contents of the room.

No stairs. Just another empty hotel room coated in a layer of dust. The standard bed, nightstand, and dresser were the only occupants of the room.

Jonah took a deep breath. It wasn't an exit, but it also didn't contain whatever lurked up here, and for that he was grateful.

But it also meant that there was a higher chance of finding the thing behind the next door.

"All clear," he whispered to Chuck.

They continued their search for an exit. The friends stopped by several rooms, not seeing anything that could help them get back down to the third floor. At one point they thought they heard something, but it turned out to be the plastic sheeting moving in the breeze.

"This place creeps me out," Chuck whispered to Jonah.

"I wouldn't be here unless it was our only choice," Jonah whispered back.

Welcome To Nightmare Island

They had gone about halfway through the hall when a light turned on behind them. The guys swung around to see that the lights had turned back on in the elevator, and the girls were smiling with relief and waving for them to join them back in the elevator.

That's when they heard it.

It started out with what sounded like dragging chains. Then they could hear its breathing. It was labored and slightly muffled.

The guys spun around, struggling to hear where the sound was coming from, but they didn't have to wait long.

As the storm raged on, a bolt of lightning lit up the sky, and in doing so, it cast its light through the hallway. The light was only there for a split second, but it was enough. In the moment of light that it provided; they had seen the dark figure at the end of the hall.

Jonah could only think to himself, if they could see the figure, it could see them. His fear drove him into action. He grabbed Chuck by the shirt and began pushing him along.

They ran headlong back toward the elevator.

The figure at the end of the hall seemed to realize what Jonah's intents were, and the sound of chains shuffling grew ever closer.

Another lightning bolt lit up the hallway, and they could see the figure was now only twenty feet away.

Annie leapt to the button panel and began slapping the third-floor button.

Kevin joined Annie at the panel and began pressing buttons. Obviously, he thought Annie wasn't doing it right, or it was the only thing he could think to do in these pressing times.

Whatever he did seemed to work. The doors began to slide shut.

As lightning lit the hallway one more time, they could see the shadowy figure was only ten feet away, but he seemed to be gaining speed. They could hear its labored breathing growing louder and louder and it seemed fervent on catching up to them. Because the window was at its back, the lightning couldn't light up the things front, so they weren't able to get a good view of the thing.

And for that, Kevin was glad. He didn't know if he could deal with seeing the face of another nightmarish thing on this island.

It was right at the heels of Chuck and Jonah as they ran. Jonah could feel the hairs on his neck rise as he went, though he wouldn't spare a moment to look back, he knew it was right on the verge of catching them. They could see the light in front of them fading as the elevator doors slowly slid shut. Jonah didn't know if they were going to make it in time. His fear sent his adrenaline pumping, and he grabbed Chuck's shirt and put on a burst of speed. They dove into the elevator just in time, sending the room into a dizzying sway.

Just as they thought the thing was going to make it into the elevator with them, the doors slammed shut.

They let out a collective sigh of relief. Their visits to the fourth floor had to stop becoming a pattern, Jonah thought to himself. Thank God they were going to be leaving tomorrow because...

That's when they heard the crash above them.

Whatever was chasing them must not have stopped when the door closed. The room shook as pieces of the fourth-floor doors shattered upon the top of the elevator. This was followed by an even louder thump.

They all stared up at the ceiling with fear in their eyes. That's when they heard the chains.

The thing from the fourth floor had followed them. It was on the roof of the elevator.

Suddenly the elevator shook with such intensity that Jonah thought they were going to plunge to their deaths.

The thing was trying to break through the ceiling.

Chuck began pressing the buttons feverishly, willing the elevator to move faster, to let them off at their destination, hell, any destination. Any floor would be good enough to get them off the elevator and away from the thing on top of it.

The elevator shook once more as the thing kicked right through the ceiling panels, knocking the light onto the floor. It crashed at their feet, shattering to pieces, and plunging them into complete darkness once more.

They stumbled around in the dark, trying to get as far away from the small opening the thing had made.

It continued to lash out at the ceiling, making an opening big enough for it to fit through.

Just when they thought they were going to be goners, the elevator dinged.

The doors slid open, and they all fell out onto the third floor. Jonah scrambled backward on his hands, looking back toward the elevator. They had made it to their floor, but they weren't safe yet.

The thing made one final kick, sending fragments of the elevator ceiling splintering to the floor.

Then it fell to the ground, landing with a thud on its feet.

Chapter Twenty

"What do you want?" Annie screamed at the thing in the elevator.

It stood hunched over in the dark room, seeming to pant as it caught its breath. Then as they watched, it began to shuffle toward them. When it finally made its way out into the light of the third-floor hallway, they all gasped in shock.

The thing chasing them wasn't a ghost at all. It was a man.

He was completely disheveled. His clothes were wrinkled and dust-covered. His face was coated in grime so thick they could see the lines in it where his skin creased. His hair was greasy and looked like it hadn't been combed in days.

Jonah felt a wave of nausea as the man's smell hit him. This dude reeked.

But the man's bathing habits weren't what immediately caught their attention. His mouth was duct taped shut, with the tape wrapping around his head several times. The edges of the tape had begun to lose their stickiness. Where the sides of the tape had begun to peel, they could see a layer of the man's face grease covering it.

Welcome To Nightmare Island

His hands and feet were chained together. Jonah thought this must be where the sounds of rattling chains had been coming from.

The skin around the man's wrists and ankles had been worn raw from struggling against his restraints. They were red and the skin had begun to peel in some places.

Jonah noticed that the man's clothes seemed to be too big on him. He must have been emaciating away up on the fourth floor before they came.

Slightly quieter this time, Annie said, "What do you want?"

The man looked at Annie, then motioned with his hands toward his face.

"I think he wants us to remove the duct tape," Jonah said.

"But what if he tries to hurt us?" Annie said.

"What's he gonna do?" Kevin shot back at her. "He's all chained up. Plus, he's so thin that if he tries something even I could take him down."

Jonah moved slowly toward the man. With his hands palms up, he approached the man like a wild animal.

"I'm going to remove the duct tape. Is that okay?" Jonah asked the man.

The man nodded his head.

"It's going to hurt a bit," Jonah said eyeing the parts of the tape that were stuck to the man's facial hair.

The man nodded again.

Jonah slowly brought his hands to the man's face, searching for the seam in the duct tape that would set the man free. Finding it, he peeled back enough of the tape to get a firm grasp on it, and he began to pull. The tape came away with a ripping noise, tearing out a few locks of the man's hair.

The man flinched but resigned to letting Jonah take the rest of the tape off. It was still looped around one more time.

Jonah pulled once more, this time taking off the layer of tape that was attached to his skin. This one seemed to come away with some of the man's beard, and the skin on his face.

The whole group seemed to flinch with that last yank of the tape.

Where Jonah had thought the tape had ripped the man's skin off, there was a band of skin that had been covered by the tape and otherwise uncovered by the layer of grease and dust that covered every other inch of the man's body.

"Ow," the man rasped out. He began to tense and relax his jaw muscles, which likely hadn't been used in a while. "Do...do any of you have any water?"

His voice was weak and dry. He probably hadn't spoken for quite some time either.

Audrey walked to their room and grabbed a bottle of water off her nightstand. She came back and tried to hand it to the man to drink.

He looked at the bottle, then at his hands, which were still chained to his feet.

"Do you mind?" he asked. "I'm a little indisposed currently."

Hesitating, she undid the cap and pressed the bottle to his lips. He seemed to have a reaction once the water entered his mouth, like a kid being given a piece of candy. He gulped and gulped at the drink.

"Easy, easy," Audrey said taking the water back. "If you drink too fast, you're only going to make yourself sick." She brought the bottle back to his lips, and he paced himself this time. When he finished the bottle, she asked, "Now who are you?"

The man cleared his throat before saying; "My name is Maverick Knight."

Chapter Twenty-One

Jonah and the rest of the group looked at the man, too stunned to speak.

The man looked around at the group before saying, "Who the hell are you and what are you doing on my island?"

"The-there was an invitation delivered to my door the other day," Jonah stammered out. "It was inviting us to spend three days on the island enjoying all the haunts it had to offer. It was addressed to me from Maverick Knight." Jonah looked confusedly at the man, who gave him a quizzical look right back.

"I didn't send you any invitation," the man said. He looked like he was puzzling over something.

"I'm sorry," Audrey said. "Did you say your name was Maverick Knight?"

"Alive and in the flesh," the man said.

"But we met Maverick Knight already," Kevin said. "We met him as soon as we stepped foot on the island. Tall guy, with long black hair."

The man seemed alarmed, before a look of recognition passed over his face.

Devin Cabrera

"That man is a fraud," the man said. "He is just one of Miles's goons. A few days ago, Miles and his henchmen snuck onto the island and attacked me. The next thing I know, I wake up bound and gagged on the fourth floor of the hotel. They had rigged the elevator panel so I couldn't call it to my floor. And this hotel didn't have stairs built into it by the time they stopped working on it. Recently I had been fussing with the wiring of the panel, trying to get it to operate how it should. But I couldn't do much good in the dark with my hands tied behind my back."

Jonah remembered the night before. The elevator had woken them all up when it had started going off by itself. That must have been the real Maverick Knight trying to escape. They had thought it had been faulty wiring or ghosts that had been causing the elevator to malfunction.

"I had almost given up on escaping, but that's when I heard the elevator coming up last night. I thought it was Miles, trying to get me to give up the location of the orb. I got ready to attack him with whatever strength I had left. But then I saw you all in the elevator. I must say I was in a state of shock. And I don't get shocked much outside of my line of work."

The real Maverick beckoned toward the water bottle in Audrey's hand once more. "Can I have some more of that?" he asked.

Audrey obliged, and the man gulped down the remainder of the bottle.

Continuing, Maverick said, "I didn't send you an invitation. Nobody should be on this island. It isn't safe. If for any reason, those barriers go down, anyone on the island is as good as dead. I didn't put those ghosts here so that I could charge admission. I put them here so I could prevent them from haunting the rest of the world. I did it to keep people like you safe from things like that."

With this, Maverick nodded his head toward the windows at the end of the hall. They didn't have to get up and look, they knew far too well what he was talking about.

Maverick looked around at the group of friends. He seemed flustered. He seemed almost as if he was more pissed by the fact that they were on the island than he was by the fact that he had been kidnapped and stored in a building with no escape.

"So, if you weren't the one that sent the invitation, who did? And why?" Jonah asked the man.

"My being kidnapped, and you having received that invitation happened too close to be a coincidence. Miles must be behind all of this. He wouldn't get an outside party involved unless he needed something from them," Maverick said. "He must think that you can help him get the orb."

Jonah's hand went instinctively to his back pocket where he always kept his pocket watch, the one that had been passed down from generation to generation. But the watch was gone.

All eyes in the group moved to him as he emptied his pockets. He was beginning to freak out.

Jonah checked every pocket he had but he turned up with nothing. He never went anywhere without that pocket watch. It was like his good luck charm. When he had wrote his first novel, that watch was on his desk. He had kept it there, with the lid open. The watch side told him when he needed to take a break or get to work. While the lid side held a photo of his parents. It was the only photo he had of them together, and it gave him a boost of confidence to think that they were watching him as he worked. He would have liked to think that they might be proud of the work that he was doing.

But now the pocket watch was gone. Besides containing the only photo of his parents that he owned, it was also the only heirloom that he had from his family that had any meaning. Yeah, he had some furniture and other knick knacks that he had inherited when his grandfather passed away, but this was the only object that held any meaning to him.

It had been passed down through generations of Peterson men and was supposed to have belonged to one of his great grandfathers. Though Jonah knew very little of the man, he was told that he was one of the very first ghost hunters. After reading about the Salem witch trials, Jonah didn't really trust the abilities of the old timers to judge what may be determined to be supernatural.

Jonah had written off the stories of his great grandfather but had kept the pocket watch all the same. As he was a horror writer, he felt like having it nearby helped to inspire him to write good stories, like a blacksmith who is given a talent in his field which was passed down to him from generation to generation.

But now the watch was gone, and Jonah was freaking out.

"What's wrong with you?" Kevin asked, a worried look passing over his face as he saw his friend pacing the hall frantically.

"I can't find my pocket watch," Jonah said.

"That old piece of junk? I told you to get rid of it and get something classier. Maybe this is God giving you a sign that you need to move on from that thing," Kevin said with a smirk.

"What did this pocket watch look like?" Maverick asked.

"It was a brass pocket watch. It had a clock face on one side and a photo of my parents under the lid. On the outside of the lid, it had my family's crest," Jonah said.

"What did the crest look like?" Maverick asked.

"It was a ram skull over a pentagram," Jonah said. "The last time I saw it was when we were leaving the library. Then I got bumped into on the way back to the hotel and Miles helped me up."

"I hate to tell you this, but I think you became the victim of a pickpocket," Chuck said.

"By who? Miles?" Jonah asked. "What would he want with my old pocket watch?"

Chapter Twenty-Two

Deep underground, Miles walked up to a pair of steel doors. Unlike the rest of the things on this island, these doors seemed brand new. They were state of the art, with a panel on the wall beside them that would allow the user to gain access. Miles pressed his palm against the doors, sizing them up. They were thick, and no amount of brute strength was going to get through them. Someone would have better luck breaking into a bank vault than breaking through these doors.

Miles sighed, though he would've liked to find a way to blast these doors out of the wall, he had a simpler option. He went over to the panel beside the door and typed in a code. With a click, an inner locking mechanism disengaged, and the doors swished open.

Miles walked into the room. It was completely empty except for a floating blue orb in the center of the room. Upon further inspection, he could make out dark black swirls moving around inside the orb.

This was the one thing powerful enough to keep the ghosts at bay. The orb was currently sending a signal to the tower above ground, about twenty feet above where Miles currently stood.

He reached his hand out to try to touch the orb, but it was as if his hand and the orb were two ends of a magnet, desperately trying to repel each other. Miles pulled his hand away; he wasn't going to get the orb as easily as that.

But he had prepared for this. He wouldn't have come to the island unless he knew exactly what to do to get his hands on the orb. It had all been planned out months ahead of time. Figuring out Maverick's code? That was the easy part. Thanks to technology these days, everything leaves a trace. He had one of his goons hack into the island's computer servers and figure out what all of Maverick's passwords were. Funny enough, the code to the orb room was his birthday.

Next, he had to figure out when Maverick would be on the island. Once again, his hacker had logged into Maverick's files and accessed his calendar. Technology really has made everything in life so much easier.

Then Miles and his goons came to the island, grabbed Maverick while he was sleeping, chained him up, and delivered him to the fourth floor of the hotel. There, they ripped out the panel that would have allowed him to call the elevator to the fourth floor. Without it, he would be stuck there to rot or jump out a window. Miles would be happy with either of Maverick's choices.

However, that still left one part of the plan out. He had to steal the orb. Unfortunately, it was inaccessible to the human touch. Not only did the orb shell out enough energy to repel anything near it, but the moment it touched human flesh, the skin would just melt off. Humans just weren't meant to handle that kind of energy.

It wasn't as simple as hacking into the computer and turning it off or finding a numerical code in a folder somewhere that would give them access to it. No, this was unlike any other security system in the world. You see, Maverick's door codes weren't that complicated because even if someone were to get into the room, they would still need something else to get the orb.

Something almost unattainable.

Almost.

Welcome To Nightmare Island

The barrier didn't work simply because of technology. It helps, but a key component that made it work was a spell spoken in the dead language. You can't contain a ghost simply from a product of our world. You must also bring in something from their world.

How would you find such a spell? That's the hard part. It would have to be obtained from speaking to a member of an ancient civilization, one that no longer exists. Or, you would have to get it from someone that was around at that time.

Miles reached into his pocket and pulled out Jonah's pocket watch.

This was the only reason he had invited Jonah and his friends to the island.

One day while he was skulking around trying to think of a way to steal the orb, he had wandered into a bookstore. On a table in the horror section was a stack of books by an author by the name of Jonah Peterson. Miles flipped the book over and there it was. Jonah's author photo contained a picture of him holding his grandfather's watch. It wouldn't have meant anything to anyone outside of the ghost business, but Miles had recognized the symbol on Jonah's watch.

He had stolen the pocket watch out of Jonah's pocket when he had bumped into him outside the hotel. Miles opened it to reveal a photo of Jonah's parents. He took a moment to examine the photo, then tore it out. From where the photo used to be, there was a message inscribed into the metal.

A message written by Jonah's great, great, great, great grandfather.

The message had been scratched into the metal of the interior of the pocket watch, but it hadn't been written in any language that most people would be able to read. It was only because Miles had been studying the dead language for years that he was able to pronounce the words inscribed there.

"Duthraka anu hippa asta mica krapa..." Miles began. He continued reading the ancient spell, which required him to repeat the words in a chant with increasing volume. "Duthraka anu hippa asta mica krapa..."

As he spoke, the light coming from the orb pulsed brighter and brighter. After several minutes of this chant, the light became almost blinding, lighting up every corner of the room and making Miles wince in pain, but he persisted.

Finally, when he thought he couldn't take much more of it, the orb's light dulled back to normal. Then, it began to float toward him. Because he was the one who had spoken the spell, it would respond to him now. As the orb reached him, Miles grabbed a case that he had specifically commissioned just for this. It was made from stainless steel and had several layers of insulation to keep any forms of light or radiation from penetrating the case. He brought the case up to the orb, letting it fall into the hollowed-out circle in the center, before snapping the case shut.

There was an immediate change in the atmosphere of the room. It seemed to grow darker and colder at the same time. It was almost as if by taking away the orb, he had single-handedly taken away any happiness that had happened on the island. His mind, which had been filled with thoughts of the money and power the orb would bring him, immediately filled with dread.

The walls of the tunnels were lined with materials meant to repel ghosts, but unless Miles was planning on staying down here, that wouldn't help him. He had to leave the island to collect the funds for the orb, but now that it had been removed, there would be nothing stopping the ghosts from getting to him once he was above ground.

He needed to get off the island.

Chapter Twenty-Three

Back at the hotel, Jonah and his friends could feel it too. The lights dimmed slightly. The hairs on the back of Jonah's neck stood up. A wave of utmost despair seemed to wash through him, and he shivered in the sudden chill.

Maverick noticed the difference as well, and a look of sheer terror crossed his face.

"Show me your wrists!" Maverick yelled at the group. He held up his own wrists as if to mime what he wanted them to do. His hands were still cuffed together and the links holding them rattled as he moved.

Jonah hesitated, slightly stunned by the man's sudden change of attitude along with the change in atmosphere. Then he held up his wrists to Maverick, and he noticed something had changed.

He brought his wrists back up to his own eyes. Was it a trick of the light, or was this really happening?

The pulsing light on his wristband had gone out.

Jonah twisted it around, looking for any signs of the light it once held, but there was nothing. It was now just a cold piece of metal dangling from his wrist.

He looked around at the rest of the group, searching for the familiar pulse of light. But there was none.

Jonah shoved the wristband in Maverick's face. "What does this mean?" Jonah asked. "Why did the light go out?"

Maverick turned away. He began to pace around the room, his cuffs rattling as he did so. Finally, he turned back to the group, a grave look on his face.

"If the light on your wristbands is out, it means that Miles has the orb." Maverick went on, "If Miles has the orb, then it means that nothing is powering the barriers. And if the barriers aren't working..."

"Then there's nothing stopping the ghosts from getting out," Jonah finished in horror.

Back at the lighthouse, Henry had seen the lights above him go out during the storm. He cursed to himself. Normally during storms like this, he liked to sit in front of the lighthouse windows and watch as the lightning lit up the sky or watch the way the patterns of rainfall changed as it hit the waters of the lake below him. It was calming to him, listening to the patter of the rain against the glass.

It reminded him of his days as a boy in Louisiana. His family had been poor, and he had spent many a day staring up at the sky as the raindrops bounced off the tin roof. There wasn't much he could do in the rain to entertain himself back then, his mother hadn't let him go outside to play fearing he would catch himself a cold. So, he enjoyed seeing the light show that the lightning provided. It had been like a free firework display just for him.

An arc of lightning lit up the sky, bringing Henry back to the present. He sighed. Though most of the problems on the island he felt could always be pushed off to a later date, power was not one of those things. After a few minutes without power, someone was bound to come find him and demand that he fixed the situation. He just wished that he didn't have to do it in the middle of the night during a storm.

Welcome To Nightmare Island

Henry trooped down the stairs, slipping on his boots and raincoat. It was going to be a wet one tonight. He picked up his toolbox and yanked open the lighthouse door, then set out into the storm.

Immediately, the calming sensation that he had felt listening to the rain hit the windows was gone. Now the rain seemed to lash at him like a whip, the hurricane-force winds seeming to pick up the droplets and throw them at him. He pushed through it one step at a time, fighting his way against the storm.

Henry was already willing for the night to be over, unfortunately, his destination was still a few hundred yards away. He kicked and fought his way through the wind and the rain until finally, he made it to the shed by the signal tower.

Henry rushed through the door, slamming it shut behind him. He slid off the hood of his raincoat before shaking some of the excess water from himself. Reaching into his toolbox, he pulled out a flashlight and clicked it on.

He squinted his eyes, trying to get used to this newfound light in the darkness. Then he found what he was looking for.

The backup generator.

Because everything on this island was ancient, the generator wouldn't automatically come on when the power went out. Instead, somebody would have to go out and manually turn it on. That somebody happened to be him currently.

He primed the gas, then yanked on the pull cord to start it up. It gurgled a few times before failing to catch. He tried again, but to no avail. Henry shined his flashlight onto the gas gauge.

"Shit," he muttered to himself. It was empty.

Thankfully he had the foresight to keep a red five-gallon jug in the shed for this very situation. Henry picked up the jug, which seemed to be about half full.

It wasn't going to last the whole night, but it might provide him with enough light to figure out where the main power went down and fix the situation.

He walked it over to the generator, placing the flashlight in his mouth while he undid the gas cap and began to pour it in. He could feel the weight of the gas in the jug begin to lessen as it dripped into the generator.

Bang! A thunderclap shook the shack so hard Henry thought a truck had driven into the side of it.

He jumped from the shock, dropping the flashlight and the gas can as he did so.

Henry bent over to pick up the flashlight and saw the gas can turned over on its side, leaking its contents all over the floor.

This whole night was just not going his way, Henry thought to himself as he bent to pick up the can. He brought it back up the generator and continued to refill it. Now there would be even less time that the generator would be operational, due to the amount of gas that had been spilled onto the floor, and Henry didn't want to be there if a lightning bolt hit the shack, because it would go up in flames faster than a barn filled with hay at this point.

He placed the gas cap on the generator and tugged at the pull cord again. This time it sprang to life, giving a loud rumble as it fired up. The shed light flickered back on above him, and Henry sheathed his flashlight back into his toolbox. His work here was done.

Making sure all his things were in order, he slid his hood back on and slipped back into the storm.

As he walked outside, he shielded his eyes from the rain. He didn't look up, but if he did, he would have noticed that the signal tower was no longer pulsing blue. In fact, it had gone completely dark. He didn't notice that his wristband was dark either because it was covered by the sleeve of his raincoat.

What he did notice, however, was that when the next flash of lightning lit up the sky, there was a shadow on the ground next to his own.

Henry stopped in his tracks. The hair on the back of his neck began to tingle. He took a deep breath, trying to work up the courage to turn around. In doing so, he inhaled the strong stench of death and decay in the air.

Welcome To Nightmare Island

He whipped around, only to see the Huntsman staring back at him, his face inches from his own.

Henry stood there, frozen, unsure of what to do. In all his time on the island, he had never seen any of the ghosts outside of their designated areas. He couldn't remember what he was supposed to do if he ran into one of them.

He managed to tear his eyes away from the Huntsman just long enough to notice that his bracelet was no longer lit up. The system was down, which meant that he was on his own out here.

Henry looked back at the Huntsman's face. It was a face of pure evil, of a man that wanted nothing but to hear Henry's body being ripped limb from limb.

Henry took a step back. In that moment, the wind died down, and the storm seemed to grow silent. In that one split second of silence, Henry heard the crunch of leaves around him, and he remembered something that he had forgotten about the Huntsman.

The Huntsman never traveled alone.

Henry whipped around just in time to see one of the Huntsman's hounds pounce toward him. He swung his flashlight toward the beast, managing to avert its attack, only to feel the jaws of another hound clench around the back of his neck, and pull him to the ground.

Chapter Twenty-Four

Back at the hotel, the group of friends were panicking. They had come to the island to have a good time. Now they've come to find out that they were at the zoo and the lions have been released. They were all in mortal danger and it was only a matter of time before they ran into something. It was a few hours before they were all supposed to leave on the first boat out in the morning, but to get to the boat, they had to cross an island filled with the most dangerous ghosts on the planet.

"So, what's our next move?" Audrey said.

"The first thing we do is find a way to get me out of these cuffs," Maverick said. "Does anyone have a hacksaw or an axe handy?"

"I have something better," Chuck said. He went into his room and brought out his duffle bag. Reaching inside, he brought out a key ring. On the keyring was an array of handcuff keys, generally able to open most sets of handcuffs. "When I'm not exploring haunted islands, I patrol the streets as a police officer. I never go anywhere without my keys; you never know what kind of situation you'll run into."

Welcome To Nightmare Island

Maverick raised his cuffed hands to Chuck, who unlocked the sets of cuffs on his hands and then his ankles.

Finally free, Maverick rubbed the skin on his wrists where it had been rubbed raw by the cuffs. He wasn't going to forget the feeling of them anytime soon.

"Right, so the way I see it, we have a couple of options," Maverick said. "Option one, we all get to the other side of the island and wait for the boat to get here at sunrise, and we all get the hell off this island. Though, with the ghosts being free, we could all die trying to get there. Option two, we track down Miles and retrieve the orb, placing it back in the signal chamber, giving us a chance to capture the ghosts again to prevent them from terrorizing the living. Though, on second thought, Miles and his goons are probably armed and will either shoot us or feed us to the ghosts if we try to get close to them." Maverick paced the room, he seemed to be thinking of ways around the obstacles at hand.

Kevin looked between his friends and Maverick. "There's a third option, right?" he said.

Maverick looked up from his pacing. "Well of course there's a third option."

Kevin seemed visibly relieved. He took a deep breath and relaxed in his seat.

"The third option is that we wait here in the hotel for rescue teams to arrive and save us," Maverick said. "However, there is no way to contact the outside world without service. And nobody in their right mind would come to this island willingly, knowing what it holds."

With this, Maverick glanced around at the members of the group, who looked sheepishly at the floor.

"No. Option three would just be to wait here until the horde of ghosts converges upon us, and we get used as their playthings before we suffer a long, drawn out, and torturous death," Maverick said glumly.

Maverick got to his feet, wobbling a little bit as he focused what remaining energy he had on not falling over.

"Get whatever you need and let's go," Maverick said to the group of friends.

They all seemed too stunned to move. An hour ago, they had all been on their way to their beds, ready to lay around restlessly until dreams about the nightmares they saw that night overtook them. Now this strange man from the fourth floor was telling them that they could all potentially die tonight.

Nothing was as it seemed. The man who they had grown to trust, the man who had been showing them around the island safely and providing an experience that they had never had before, had lied and stolen from them. They had been used to gain access to the orb, and now if they didn't make it to the boat on time, they would surely die.

"Let's go!" Maverick yelled. "I'm not planning on dying in this hotel, and if you aren't ready to go in five minutes, you will be left behind."

This jolted the friends into action. They all ran to their rooms, only grabbing what they thought they would need to make it to the other side of the island. A warm jacket, flashlights, a few bottles of water... What could you use to potentially fight off a murderous ghost? Could you fight them?

One by one, they each filed back into the hallway, where they found Maverick pacing the room.

"We need to get to the other side of the island. There we can hopefully wait out the storm and hide from the ghosts long enough for the boat to arrive. Then we can get the hell out of here," Maverick said.

He led the way over to the elevator, waiting for the group to follow. They hesitated, if only for a second. The last time they were in this elevator, they were terrified for their lives that a ghost was going to barge through the ceiling, but it had turned out only to be Maverick.

Welcome To Nightmare Island

They followed him inside, kicking pieces of rubble away to make room for all of them.

Jonah looked up through the hole that Maverick had made in the ceiling. There was nothing but inky blackness above them, and he could imagine that that was what awaited them on the lower half of the shaft as well, along with a three-story drop to their deaths.

The group squeezed into the elevator, before pressing the L button for the lobby. They had to clear even more of the debris out of the way to let the door close. Finally, the door closed with a ding, and the elevator began its descent, screaming in protest the entire way.

Jonah hoped that Maverick jumping on the elevator and destroying its ceiling wouldn't throw off the system enough to send them plunging to the ground. He didn't want to think about that, so he changed the subject.

"So Maverick, if Miles isn't really a tour guide for the island, who is he?" Jonah asked.

"He used to be my partner," Maverick replied. He stared off into the distance as if remembering something from long ago. "We used to hunt ghosts together. We would watch each other's backs, and make sure we didn't get killed. Ghost hunting was a lucrative business, as you can imagine. A lot of times, when a residence becomes haunted, and the ghosts start going after the family members, it strikes an animalistic fear in the hearts of men. This fear drives men to the point where they would do anything or even pay anything to get rid of the problem and get their lives back to normal. Other times, we would get called in by the Vatican itself, to deal with the more dangerous ghosts. And you know how much money the church has in its coffers. A seemingly endless supply. When God didn't answer people's prayers to keep them safe, the church called us. Eventually, I used some of the funds I made from ghost hunting to develop the orb. It combined today's technology with a spell from the dead language. Using it, I was able to capture the worst ghosts and transport them to a different location. This location."

He looked around at the rest of the group to make sure they were paying attention. They were.

He continued. "With this technology, we became the best ghost hunters in the world. Some ghosts are just too powerful to be exorcised and sent back to hell. With the power of the orb, we were able to capture even those, and they are the ones you've seen around the island. We were singlehandedly putting other ghost hunters out of business. Everyone else in the business wanted to get their hands on the orb, and they would be willing to pay a hefty price for it. Miles thought that we should sell it, take the money, and retire. But we already had more money than we knew what to do with. He just wanted more. I refused to sell the orb. Doing so could put the control of the most dangerous army of lost souls into the hands of someone who could use it for no good. I wouldn't have that. We fought about it for months, and eventually, we broke apart. To this day, he has been trying to get his hands on the orb. But even if he had gotten to the orb, he wouldn't have been able to remove it without reading the spell in the dead language. The spell which only I knew. I had never shared it with him, and it drove Miles mad that I refused to tell it to him." He sighed and looked at the ground. "Somehow, it appears that he has gained access to the spell."

They all took a moment to think about how Miles having the orb would affect them. For one thing, they would likely die on this island like the people who lived here during the asylum outbreak. Then the ghosts would likely leave the island and wreak havoc on the rest of the world. Without having the orb to capture the ghosts, their reign of terror may go on for eternity.

The silence was broken by the ding of the elevator. They had reached the lobby. This was the moment of truth. For all they knew, the ghosts could be lined up outside the elevator doors waiting to get a shot at tearing them apart.

They waited with bated breath as the doors slid slowly open, revealing... Nothing. The hotel lobby was completely empty.

Jonah released a breath. He was sure the ghosts would already be here. Maybe they hadn't realized yet that the barrier had failed.

Then a grislier thought hit him. Maybe they hadn't gone after the group of friends yet because they were busy with the other people on the island. He shuddered. He didn't want to think about what the ghosts would do to the other people on the island, because it would just be a sneak peek of what they would do to him and his friends eventually. He worried for Henry's safety, as well as for Miles. Though the man was a bad guy, nobody deserved what would happen if one of these ghosts ran into them.

Then he remembered something.

Turning to Maverick he asked, "Are there any ghosts in this hotel?"

Maverick looked at Jonah. "What do you mean?"

Jonah glanced at his friends briefly before responding. "Each night that I've been here, I've dreamt of ghosts in the hotel." He went on to describe the ghosts that he had seen in his waking nightmares.

Maverick looked down at the floor. Apparently, he was no stranger to these ghosts that seemed to roam freely in their dreams. "Those ghosts are just as real as the ones you saw on your tour. Though not quite evil enough to embody a physical form like the others. What you saw were the island's memories. This island seems to remember the horrible things that happened here, and it tends to play those memories back repeatedly like an echo. That's what most ghost encounters consist of, however, this island seems to be chock full of memories of tragic things. That's the one fault of the orb. It can only protect you from ghosts that wish to do you harm. However, it has no control over the ghosts of our past."

"So, the ghosts that I saw in the hotel room," Jonah began. "That stuff really happened?"

Maverick nodded solemnly.

Jonah gulped. He thought back to the night when he saw the ghost of the inmate slamming the nurse's head against the door repeatedly. That was an image that was going to run through his mind until the day he died. Unfortunately, that day might be today.

Chapter Twenty-Five

Maverick grabbed the door handle, bracing himself for the outside world. He looked back to make sure that everyone else was ready. Sure that they were as ready as they would ever be, he took a deep breath and opened the front door of the hotel.

Immediately they were met with a strong gust of wind. The storm still raged on outside. Droplets of rain stung their faces as the wind seemed to throw itself in their direction.

Then, they ran out in the storm in the direction of the other side of the island.

Jonah became soaked to the bone immediately after stepping outside. Mother nature was going to have its way with them tonight. He ran with all his might, trying to follow Maverick in the inky black darkness. It was extremely hard to see in front of him. Between it being the dead of night, plus with the rain forcibly attacking his eyelids, he could barely make out anything in front of him. Had he been able to see properly, he wouldn't have stepped in the pothole filled with water. Instantly he could feel his shoe fill with rainwater. Then his toe caught the lip of the hole, and he went down. He scraped his knee on the cobblestones as he fell, cursing himself for being so stupid as to not look where he was going.

He didn't have enough time to warn the rest of his friends though, none of which could see him sprawled out on the ground. He felt a rush of pain as Chuck stepped on him before falling himself. Then the rest of the group tumbled down upon him.

If this was how the night was going to go, it was going to be a very long night.

He looked up at the sky, just as a lightning bolt arced across it. What he saw terrified him to his very core.

Lit up very briefly by the lightning, he could see a ghost lumbering toward them.

It must have been about fifty feet away from them. He didn't have time to see which one it was, but he knew they needed to move.

Jonah shouted at his crew. "Get up! There's a ghost coming toward us!"

They scrambled to their feet, the presence of a ghost filling them with adrenaline.

Jonah could make out the shape of a building nearby. "This way!" he shouted over the storm, pulling Audrey in the direction of the building.

They raced toward it, even faster than they had before. Reaching the door, Jonah pulled it open, struggling with the force of the wind trying to push it closed. They all rushed in, slamming the door shut behind them and bracing it shut with a nearby board.

Jonah bent over, catching his breath. Now that he could think, he realized that he hadn't run since high school. He should really get back into the habit of doing so to stay in shape.

He decided to count the heads in the room. He turned his flashlight on and swept it around at his friends. Chuck, Audrey, Kevin, Annie... That was it.

"Where's Maverick?" He asked the group.

"You were the one behind him," Kevin said.

Jonah realized Kevin was right. Maverick had been leading the charge. When Jonah had fallen, Maverick had kept going without them. With the noise from the storm, he probably hadn't heard them all falling behind. They had been separated, and he wouldn't have known where they had gone. Even worse, he was out there with that ghost.

Now they had been separated from the only man on this island they thought they could trust, the only one who knew what was going on and could possibly lead them to safety.

Jonah turned away from the door, and what he saw made him gulp in fear.

They were in the infirmary. The one that they had visited on the first night of their tour. This was the building where they had first witnessed real ghosts, and they had just barricaded themselves inside with them.

"Shush," Jonah said to his friends. They all grew silent, taking in their surroundings. Realizing where they were, they all began to listen for any sounds of movement in the halls. After a few moments without any sound to be heard other than the pounding rain outside, Jonah decided it was time to do something.

They could either leave through the door they had come in, and get killed by the ghost outside, or they could try to make their way to one of the other exits without disturbing the ghosts inside. Option two was the only one that left them with a chance of getting out alive, so he decided to go with that one.

"Follow me," Jonah said pointing his flashlight down the hallway in front of him. He could see the blood trails they had walked past the day before. He knew that the trails led to the enclosure where Bertha and her child were kept. If they kept quiet as they went by, the ghosts might not notice them. Or at least, so he hoped.

His friends followed behind him, none of them wanting to get split up again. As the trail of blood wound its way through the halls, they saw where the trail ended. It went right through the double doors that led to the first ghost enclosure.

Jonah turned his flashlight off, doing everything he could to not be seen or heard. He crept so slowly it must have taken him several minutes to place each foot in front of the other. But even though he moved as quietly as he could, he still couldn't hear anything from the other side of the door.

Maybe the ghosts had left. Maybe they had noticed that they were no longer trapped and had decided to leave the building.

Jonah's thoughts began to be so uplifting that he began to get careless. Finally, as he began to walk in front of the double doors, he couldn't help himself any longer. He had to know if they were in there. He raised his head ever so slowly toward the glass windows set in the doors.

Audrey tugged at his shirt as he did so. "What are you doing?" she whispered emphatically.

"I need to know if they are in there!" Jonah whispered back. He continued to raise his head until finally he inched his eyes over the edge of the glass and saw... nothing. They weren't there.

Jonah let out a sigh of relief. Turning to his friends, he said: "The coast is clear, they aren't there."

But then, if they weren't in their room, where were they? Were they outside the building hunting them? Or were they roaming the halls of the building?

They didn't have to wait very long to find out.

Chapter Twenty-Six

The silence around them was shattered as the door to the infirmary flew open, crashing against the walls and splintering apart.

They all spun around in time to see the Huntsman lit up in the doorway by a flash of lightning. In his hand, he held the leashes to each of his hounds. His eyes appeared to know exactly where to look, as they seemed to peer directly into the souls of each of the scared friends.

The Huntsman took one step into the hallway, his hounds drooling with the excitement of a fresh meal. The nails on each of their mangled paws scratched the linoleum floor as the dogs fought against his grasp, eager to go after their newest prey.

Jonah and his friends stood stock still, unable to breathe, eyes locked on the ghosts, not sure what to do. The Huntsman, in turn, stared back at them, creating a silent standoff between the two parties to see who was going to move first.

It was one of the hounds.

The vicious corpse canine let out a loud growling bark, startling the friends into action.

Welcome To Nightmare Island

They raced to their feet, struggling to gain purchase on the slippery linoleum floor beneath them. They had to find a way out of the infirmary without getting eaten alive by the hounds. But right now, the way that they had come in was blocked by the bloodthirsty ghosts.

Back at the front door, the Huntsman released his hold on the hounds. In an instant, the dogs leapt toward the friends at the end of the hall, each canine picking out a target to take down.

Meanwhile, Jonah and his friends were trying to put as much distance between themselves and the dogs as possible. Chuck found a door that led to the stairwell, and he pushed it open.

"Go, go, go!" Chuck yelled, holding the door open for the rest of the group. He could hear the dogs getting ever closer with each passing second. Finally, Kevin crossed through the door, and Chuck slammed it shut. As his friends raced up the stairs, Chuck used the weight of his body to hold the door closed.

Suddenly, he felt the body of the first canine slam into the door, throwing him back a little bit.

These dogs were stronger than he thought. And a bit stupider. Being dead, they didn't have to worry about injuring themselves going after prey. What was the worst that was gonna happen?

Chuck knew then that he couldn't hold the door forever. The dogs would just keep lashing out at the door until he ran out of energy to hold it. He looked around, searching for anything that could help his cause. Looking down, he saw something he could use.

Beside the door, there was an old-fashioned radiator built into the wall.

Reaching into his pocket, Chuck pulled out the pair of handcuffs he had gotten off Maverick. He had pocketed them, not knowing if they would be of use tonight. He was glad he had thought to do so.

Chuck braced himself against the door as another volley of attacks came from the other side. With his back against it, Chuck reached down, attaching one end of the cuffs around the door handle.

Another push from behind him. The advances on the door were

coming faster now, all the dogs must now be trying to burst through the entranceway.

Chuck took the other end of the cuffs, trying to reach the radiator while still pressing his weight against the door. He had to bend down to do so, relying on the weight from his lower half to hold it closed.

Just then, the head of an axe ripped through the door where the back of his skull was just a second ago.

Chuck managed to clip the other end of the cuffs around the radiator, then quickly stepped away.

The wood splintered as the axe hammered into it once more. The Huntsman himself must be trying to break through, Chuck thought.

At this rate, it wouldn't buy them much time.

Chuck turned around and raced up the steps to catch up to his friends.

Chapter Twenty-Seven

Upstairs, Jonah and his friends had been searching frantically for a way out. They had gone from room to room, looking for a door or an elevator or another set of stairs.

"Hadn't anyone thought about fire escapes when this place was built?" Kevin asked, not really expecting anyone to answer.

Just then, Chuck burst up the stairs.

"I slowed them down, but the Huntsman is hacking through the door as we speak. We don't have much time. Find a way out yet?" Chuck asked.

"Nothing yet," Jonah replied with a nervous look on his face.

"I may have something!" Audrey called suddenly from a room down the hall.

The friends raced into the room, eager to find a way out of this building.

"It's not a door, but there's a chance it could work," Audrey said pointing to a window.

Jonah looked outside. Below the window, a metal awning sprawled over where the back door was on the floor below.

"It's probably our best shot at this point," Jonah said. He groped around for a window latch but couldn't find one. This window was meant to stay shut. "Stand back," Jonah said.

The group did as they were told. Jonah grabbed his heavy flashlight and using the butt end, he began to bust the glass out of the window, creating an opening big enough for them to crawl through.

"After you," Jonah said motioning to Annie.

Normally he wouldn't tell one of the girls to climb out of a window first, but with the building being super old and the awning made of rusted metal, it would be best for the lightest person in the group to test it out first.

Annie moved toward the window, but before she could climb out, Chuck grabbed her hand.

"Be careful," Chuck said, pulling Annie close.

"I will," Annie said into his shoulder. Then she pulled away, holding onto the window frame as she stepped out onto the structure. Her feet landed with a clang on the rusted tin roof. It was several feet below the window frame, and the whole structure shook as she met it. Steadying herself, she walked around the surface, testing her weight. It wasn't ideal, but it would have to do. She walked over to the sloped edge, trying to find where the supports were connected. Once she located them, she swung her body out over the void, relying on her upper body strength to allow her to hold onto the edge of the awning and then proceed to wrap her legs around the support pole. Annie then shimmied down the pole to the ground.

"I made it!" She called out to her friends at the window.

"Good, Audrey you go next," Jonah said.

Audrey made her way out of the window, trying to follow Annie's moves exactly.

Just then, the boys heard a noise coming from the other end of the building.

The hounds had gotten through the door and were making their way up the stairs.

Chapter Twenty-Eight

"Shit!" Chuck said.

"Go, go, go!" Jonah said pushing Kevin out the window. They no longer had time to play it safe. If they didn't make it out of there fast, they were going to become a dog's chew toy.

Audrey hadn't made it to the ground yet when she felt the awning begin to shake. Looking up from where she stood hanging onto the edge of the roof, she saw Chuck climbing out of the window to join Kevin. She didn't know much about architecture, but she knew that there was too much weight on this thing. She rushed to meet Annie on the ground.

Inside the room, Jonah could hear the dogs getting closer. He listened to the panting as they scrambled to catch up with their prey. Jonah pushed Chuck the rest of the way out of the window but hesitated to climb out after him. He knew that if too many people stood on the structure, it may collapse under their weight.

No, rushing into this could only harm them. He needed to bide his time and let some of the others descend the awning before he went out there.

Jonah thought that maybe he could barricade the door. He ran over, slamming the door shut, only to realize with horror that it didn't have a handle. Looking around, he tried to find something heavy to put in front of the door, but the room was empty.

He had run out of time. He could already feel the dogs jumping on the door, and there was nothing in place to keep it shut other than his own weight. Jonah, unfortunately, did not have the build that Chuck had, so he wouldn't be able to hold the door any longer.

"We're down!" Chuck called up to Jonah. He had just made it to the ground and was checking over the rest of his friends to make sure they didn't hurt themselves coming down. He waited, but Jonah still hadn't come to the window. He was beginning to worry about his friend. Had the dogs gotten to him?

Up in the room, Jonah was doing some mental math in his head. The window was about ten feet away from the door. He would need to let go of it and get to the window faster than the dogs.

It was now or never.

Jonah leapt away from the door just as the dogs burst through it. He ran as fast as he could across the room, the dogs nipping at his heels as he went. Using up a surge of energy he didn't know that he had, Jonah dove headfirst through the window, slicing his arms up on a piece of broken glass that clung to the edge of the frame. With a thud, Jonah's body hit the edge of the tin roof, and he kept moving.

The momentum of his dive carried him in an unstoppable slide toward the edge of the roof. He reached out for anything to stop his trajectory, anything at all, but there was nothing. Jonah slid right off the edge.

With one last ditch effort, he managed to catch the edge of the rusted canopy, stopping him mid-fall. He cried out with pain as his arms struggled to hold his weight. Blood dripped down his arms into his face.

But that was the least of his worries. All the recent stress on the awning broke it away from the wall, and Jonah could feel the tin sheets in his hands become weightless as the structure collapsed in on itself, dragging him down to the ground with it.

Chapter Twenty-Nine

Jonah's world went black. All he could see was darkness around him, and his body ached in places he didn't know could. Then Chuck and Kevin removed the sheets of tin blocking his view of the sky.

"Are you alright?" Chuck asked, pulling Jonah out of the wreckage of the awning.

"I think so," Jonah said, checking himself over. A few new scrapes and bruises, but he would be fine. He looked back up toward where he fell from, and what he saw reminded him why he had taken the plunge.

A single hound stood with its paws on the edge of the window, with another trying to squeeze its way alongside it.

"Oh shit," Jonah said struggling to his feet.

As the others followed his gaze, the first hound sprang from the windowsill, having seemingly no worries about hurting itself from falling two stories to the ground. Its body hit the earth with a thud, not quite the most graceful fall.

As the hound steadied itself back on its feet, the friends decided to take this time to get the hell out of dodge. Together, they ran into the storm.

They could hear the other hounds follow the first out the window and knew that they would soon be chased once more by the bloodthirsty demons.

"Let's go!" Chuck said from the front of the pack.

Jonah, having been weakened by his fall, could immediately feel himself falling behind. He could see Chuck's body slowly disappear into the murky fog around them.

Audrey's body wasn't built for all the running that they had been doing today, and she didn't feel very good operating under the pressure of impending death either. But she kept trucking along. Even after she had lost sight of all the people in front of her due to the fog, she told herself she had to keep moving. She couldn't see where she was going at all, but she had to focus on putting as much distance between herself and those dogs as possible.

Kevin would follow Chuck if he could. But Chuck was a police officer, and his body was trained to be able to run long distances at a time. Kevin was not. And the fact that he was a head shorter than Chuck meant that he had to struggle to keep up with each one of his giant strides.

At one point, through the sound of the rain coming down around them, Kevin thought he could hear a snarl to his right. Fearing that one of the hounds was next to him, he veered to the left to get as far away from the thing as possible.

Annie had never been so afraid in her life. She ran as fast as she could, unable to see much in the pouring rain. At one point she felt her shoe get sucked into the mud, taking it clean off her foot. Knowing that she couldn't leave the shoe behind, she went back and got it. She would run much slower without it.

As she slipped her shoe back on, she looked up, but none of her friends were visible. She took a deep breath and pushed on into the storm. The sounds of the hounds barking off in the distance were the only thing that drove her to keep moving forward. She would have to meet up with her friends later.

Annie was on her own.

Chapter Thirty

Kevin was out of breath. His lungs were on fire and there was a pain in his side that wouldn't ebb. He slowed down, listening for the sound of the dogs behind him.

He couldn't hear anything. This frightened Kevin. He couldn't hear the dogs, but he also couldn't hear his friends. He was stranded in the storm, in the dark, alone on an island with ghosts who were trying to kill him.

Kevin looked around, trying to find a familiar sight. In the distance, he could see a dark tower up ahead with a shed at its base. He began to trot toward it. It might be full of ghosts, or it might not. Anything was better than being outside in the rain with a bunch of hungry devil dogs.

He was almost to the base of the tower when he heard rustling leaves nearby. Kevin stopped where he stood, closing his eyes. He held his breath trying to remain as quiet as possible.

In his mind, he was already dead. The hounds had managed to catch up to him, and they would rip him to shreds at any moment. He thought back to when he was younger, and his dad had taken him camping for the weekend. While in the woods, his biggest fear was

Welcome To Nightmare Island

what would happen if a bear tried to eat him. His dad had reassured him, saying that if he ever encountered a bear, the best thing to do was to stand still and the bear would go away.

Kevin was trying to follow that same rule here, though he didn't know if the same rules applied to dead dogs that snacked on human flesh. He listened closely, trying to hear any sounds at all. He concentrated to the point where his mind began to create the snarls of dogs out in the distance.

Then he heard another noise.

His eyes snapped open, and turned his head to see...

"Annie?" Kevin exclaimed.

Annie was walking slowly up to Kevin, who had never been happier to see his friend's girlfriend.

Annie looked around, breathing heavily. "Have you seen any of the others?" she asked.

"No, you're the first one I've seen," Kevin replied. "Do you think any of the hounds got to them?"

"I don't even want to think about that," Annie said. "So, what is this building?" With this, she pointed at the tower above them.

"I don't know. I was just about to check it out myself."

The duo began walking toward the shed at the base of the tower. They were almost to it when Kevin tripped over something big.

He fell to the ground, cursing at whatever was in his way. He picked up his flashlight that he had dropped and shone it at the thing on the ground.

What he saw made him scurry backward.

There was a body on the ground.

"Jesus Christ!" Kevin shouted.

"Shut up, something will hear you," Annie said. She walked closer to the body, shining her light on its face. Upon seeing it, she frowned with recognition.

"Who is it? Does he look familiar to you?" Kevin asked.

"Yes. It's Henry, the lighthouse keeper," Annie replied.

Kevin made his way over to Henry. Together, they combed over his body, trying to find a pulse, but it was clear they weren't going to find any.

His entire body was covered in blood. This was due to the many gashes and bite marks that had clearly been made by the hounds. His eyes were still wide open, frozen forever in fear. One arm had been torn off completely, leaving a puddle of red on the ground beneath him.

"We can't leave him here," Annie said.

"What do you think we should do? Bury him? The things that killed him are out there right now patrolling the island trying to find us and make us look just like him. Report it to the authorities? We don't exactly know who's in charge here, and the people who are in charge probably want us dead too. No, there's nothing we can do for him now. Maybe when we get home, we can tell somebody, but right now we need to meet up with our friends and get the hell off this island," Kevin said.

Annie didn't like it, but what Kevin said was true. They had to keep moving. She reached out to Henry's face and gently pushed his lids closed.

"Come on, let's find the others," Kevin said.

Chapter Thirty-One

Chuck and Audrey had managed to catch up to each other in the storm. Stopping to take a breath, they couldn't find any of their friends nearby. So, they had decided to go into the first building they saw. This turned out to be the asylum.

"We have to be safe with every decision we make now that the ghosts have been set free," Chuck said. He tried to put his police training to use and think critically. "Maybe the others have gotten together already. And if there's one thing I know about Jonah, it's that he's smart. With the Huntsman and his hounds out there chasing us, we do know one thing, and I'm sure Jonah probably figured it out too."

"What's that?" Audrey asked.

"If the Huntsman and his hounds are outside, then they aren't in the morgue, where they used to be imprisoned. And they probably aren't likely to go anywhere near there. In fact, I'm sure they would distance themselves as far away as possible from that place to avoid getting trapped there again."

Audrey couldn't argue with that logic, so she let Chuck lead the way back to the morgue. Together, they followed the blood trails to the room where the bodies would normally be taken to be processed after death. Normally, in any horror movie that she had watched in the past, this was the kind of place that the main characters would go and would eventually be killed by the ghosts that lurked there. She and Chuck were hoping that, for once, this was the kind of place that the ghosts wanted to stay far away from.

They reached the double doors standing between them and the morgue.

"You ready for this?" Chuck asked.

Audrey took a deep breath. "I hope you're right about this."

With that, Chuck pushed open the doors to reveal...nothing. There was nobody in the morgue.

They both let out a collective sigh of relief.

Audrey walked over to the spot where they had last seen the Huntsman and his hounds occupying this room. Less than 24 hours ago, a murderous ghost and his hungry pets had been standing in this very spot. And Audrey and her friends had gawked at them like they were zoo animals. But now, the lions were out. And they were hungry.

Chuck paced back and forth. He really hoped that he was right about the others finding their way to the morgue. His girlfriend was one of the ones stuck out there with the dogs. He really didn't want to have to go back out there to find them, but he would if he had to. No, he had to at least give the others a chance to get here first. He needed to find a way to distract himself, to keep his mind off the fact that his friends might be in harm's way.

Chuck looked around. The room was set up like a typical morgue. There was a rolling chalkboard in the corner. And a counter with a ton of cabinets underneath which probably housed the coroners' tools. On the other side of the room, an entire wall was dedicated to the compartments that were meant to hold the bodies of the dead while they waited to be autopsied.

Chuck walked over to the wall. He had always seen this wall on all the true crime shows but he had always wanted to know what it looked like inside. He supposed that it had a refrigeration component inside which kept the bodies cold so that they would last long enough to be examined without rotting. He wondered if any of that still worked.

Without thinking, Chuck reached up and grabbed the handle of one of the compartments. The steel handle was cold to the touch, and the feel of it made a shiver run up his spine. With a tug, he yanked open the compartment.

"Jesus!" Chuck said, jumping back in alarm.

The steel tray inside the compartment reacted on a spring-loaded system. As Chuck opened the door, the tray shot out to meet him. This tool probably came in handy when the body on the tray belonged to a person of the heavier sort.

But the automatic tray wasn't what freaked Chuck out.

It was the body that lay on it.

Chapter Thirty-Two

"What the hell are you doing?" Audrey asked. She began to walk over to Chuck but then stopped when she saw the body on the tray.

It was the body of a man. His skin was a shade of pale white like all the blood had drained out of him. From the looks of it, his body had been cut apart and sewn back together. It was as if he had been autopsied already and then put back together in preparation for a funeral with his loved ones. Except there shouldn't be any bodies on the island.

"Maybe this guy died on the last day this place was open. And with the riots that happened here, maybe his body got left here, forgotten forever in this cubby," Audrey said.

"That would make sense, but the island had supposedly been closed for years before Maverick showed up," Chuck said. "If that were true, this body should have long decomposed."

"Maybe the same evil that allows ghosts to exist here also prevents bodies from decomposing too much," Audrey suggested.

For some odd reason, Chuck felt the urge to reach out and poke the dead man's arm. Though he had spent the last few years in law enforcement, he had normally dealt with traffic violations and had never actually seen a dead body this close.

He reached his hand out to the body.

"What are you doing?" Audrey asked.

"Relax, I just want to see what it feels like," Chuck responded.

His fingers moved to where the body's arm was, but they went right through it.

"What the..." Chuck muttered.

Suddenly, the man on the table opened his eyes. They darted around, looking first to Chuck, and then to Audrey.

Chuck jumped backward, as the man began to crawl slowly out of the tray onto the floor.

Audrey took a deep breath. "It must be a ghost," she said. "Maverick had mentioned that the island tended to remember the bad things that happened here. Without the orb doing its thing, it isn't suppressing these things as much as it should be."

The ghost got to its feet and began to limp slowly toward Chuck and Audrey. The limp seemed to be caused by a giant stab wound in the man's thigh. As he walked, they could hear the man's toe tag scraping the floor.

Krrr. Krrr.

The sound of the tags made a chill run up their spines.

The two friends didn't know what to do. They stood stock still, unable to breathe, unable to move. As the dead man began to walk closer to them, they heard a latch popping open, and then another. One by one, the compartment doors along the wall shot open, revealing trays filled with bodies in varying states of decomposition.

As they watched in horror, bodies upon bodies began to tumble out of the compartments and began walking toward them.

"We need to get the hell out of here," Chuck said to Audrey.

As they turned to run, they came face to face with Javier.

The two friends stopped dead. Their blood ran cold as they saw the face of the murderous ghost.

Javier paced toward them, looking around the room, as if

enjoying his newfound ability to walk somewhere outside his recent cell in Graystone Manor. He stretched his muscles, then ran his hand along the top of his bare scalp. Now that the barrier was no longer holding him back, he could test out some other things he hadn't been able to do for years.

He looked past Chuck and Audrey at the ghosts behind them. Seeing no threat to himself, he began to step closer to the friends, who seemed incapable of movement out of sheer terror.

"Please, please don't hurt us," Audrey begged. "We'll get off this island and never bother you again."

Javier looked down at Audrey in disdain, then switched his gaze over to Chuck, seeming to size him up with his eyes.

Javier grinned a sly devilish smile. Then he locked eyes with Chuck. His coal-black eyes bore into Chuck's own and the only thing that Chuck could think of were the dark black depths of hell.

And murder. Hatred. Outright outrage.

Chuck felt an energy come over him that he had never felt before in his life. Like he had just taken a hundred shots of adrenaline and needed something to unleash this energy on. He turned to his side, seeing something that would work just fine.

Audrey stared back at Chuck, whose smile had just turned up a notch. "Chuck, what are you doing?" Audrey asked, backing away slowly from her friend.

Chuck's eyes had grown black, mirroring those of Javier, who stood a few feet away, watching like it was an episode of his favorite show.

Audrey watched as Chuck walked across the room toward the counter. There, he bent over and began to search the drawers and cabinets. He pulled out bags and needles, gauze, and other objects the coroners would use in this room. As he picked up each item, he shook his head, tossing the objects across the room. Finally, he opened a drawer and stopped his frantic searching.

From her spot across the room, Audrey could see a row of shiny metal objects in the drawer.

Welcome To Nightmare Island

Chuck reached inside, pulling out a bone saw. He examined it slowly, turning it over in his hands before testing the sharpness of the blade against one of his fingers.

Audrey yelped as Chuck sliced open one of his fingers, enough to draw blood but not enough to sever the finger. "What are you doing?" Audrey screamed at her friend. "Stop that!"

Chuck seemed disappointed in the instrument. He dropped it back into the drawer below, and reached back inside, drawing out a shiny metal scalpel.

A smile fell across his face once more.

Chuck closed the drawer, then turned around. Locking eyes with Audrey, he began to advance toward her, scalpel raised in front of himself.

"What are you doing with that?" Audrey asked. She looked him in the eyes, noting how dark they had become. She looked back at Javier, who seemed to be enjoying this spectacle. Then she remembered something Miles had said when they toured Javier's cell.

Javier had the power to turn people. To make someone turn around and murder every one of their friends and family. This must be his doing. Chuck was under the control of Javier. And if that were true, that meant...

That Chuck was about to kill her.

Chapter Thirty-Three

"Chuck, snap out of it, man!" Audrey said. "I don't know what this asshole did to you, but you have to snap out of it."

She was taking a few steps backward as she did so, as Chuck advanced slowly toward her with no recognition in his eyes.

"You don't want to do this, Chuck!" Audrey screamed. She yelped, startled as she backed into something. It was the wall behind her. There was nowhere else to go. She was trapped with a wall behind her, a homicidal ghost to her left, the ghosts of the dead to her right, and directly in front of her was her friend who had apparently somehow been hypnotized to kill her. And the space between them was growing ever smaller.

Audrey looked around, trying to find anything that she could use to defend herself. But there was nothing. She also didn't want to hurt Chuck, but she knew that if she couldn't get him to stop, his policeman's frame would ultimately overpower her.

She tried to beg him one more time. Audrey looked Chuck right in those soulless black eyes.

"You don't have to do this Chuck, I'm your friend, Audrey. Do you remember me, Chuck? Do you remember that we are friends? You wouldn't want to hurt your friends, would you?" Audrey raised up her arms to block her face.

Chuck paused suddenly.

He was so close to Audrey that she could feel his deep ragged breaths on her face.

Audrey stood still, waiting for death to overtake her. When it didn't, she slowly brought down her arms. Chuck was directly in front of her, scalpel to his side.

Was she safe? Had she gotten through to him?

No.

Chuck smiled. An evil, malicious smile that said that he would enjoy this. Then he swung the scalpel at Audrey.

Audrey ducked, just narrowly missing the blade above her. The scalpel scraped the concrete wall where her head just was, creating a volley of sparks that rained down upon her.

She seized her chance to get away, ducking under Chuck's arm as he swung and ran past him. The look of annoyance on Javier's face as she ran past him filled her with an extra bit of energy she didn't know she had. She gave him the finger as she ran out the door of the morgue.

Clearly, Javier wasn't used to his victims getting away.

As she ran out, she could hear Chuck's lumbering steps behind her. She was athletic, but she knew that Chuck was trained to chase after perps, and she would likely be no match for him. Running wouldn't be an option, she had to hide.

Chapter Thirty-Four

Kevin and Annie made their way quietly through the fog. They left Henry's body behind and decided that the best solution would be to meet up with their friends. If they were going to get off this island, they were going to do it together, or not at all. Preferably the first one.

The problem was, they couldn't garner a sense of direction on the island during the daytime. But at night, while the fog distorted their vision and a storm raged overhead? It was damn near impossible.

The other problem that they faced was that they had no idea where their friends were. They could be in any of the surrounding buildings, or none. The worst-case scenario was that they had been captured by the Huntsman and his hounds and that their bodies were strewn around the island like the way they had just found Henry's.

Annie didn't want to think about that. Her mind was set on the task at hand. A search and rescue mission. Though her boyfriend was the one who had become a cop, he had come home many days and relayed the day's happenings to her, which made her feel like she had a sort of secondhand knowledge of police work.

She kept thinking to herself, what would Chuck do? Chuck

would probably go from building to building, making sure that each was clear of occupants before moving on to the next. Eventually, they would run into their friends somewhere.

Suddenly, Annie heard a noise behind her, like a rustle of leaves. She whipped around, expecting to have the fight of her life as a hound leaped out of the fog to take her down. But it was only Kevin, who stopped moving, wondering why Annie had swung around so fast.

She had completely forgotten that he was there. Her thoughts were elsewhere entirely.

"Shh," Annie said, putting a finger to her lips.

"Sorry," Kevin whispered. "If the dogs are nearby, we would probably smell them like a dead skunk on the side of the road. Until then, relax a little bit. Being this tense will only lead to us making a mistake."

They kept walking, not making another sound until they saw a building looming in the fog. They moved closer to it until they could make out which one it was.

"It's Graystone Manor," Annie said. "Do you think they would have gone in there?"

"I wouldn't have. That's one of the creepier places on the island. And Javier is upstairs. Why would they want to be close to that?" Kevin asked.

"Well, if the rest of the barriers are down, it's probably safe to say that Javier left his place upstairs," Annie said.

"I don't know, I don't have a very good feeling about this," Kevin said.

Just then, Annie saw a figure at the third-floor window. It was dark and foggy, so she couldn't make out who it was, but it appeared to be feminine. And the only other female she knew on the island was...

"Audrey!" Annie exclaimed. As she watched, the figure seemed to beckon them inside.

"I think I see Audrey; she's telling us to come inside," Annie said rushing off toward the house.

Kevin followed her, not looking forward to going back inside the cursed house.

Annie took the porch stairs two at a time. She was so excited to meet back up with her friends that she didn't care how much noise she made. When she saw Chuck again, she was gonna hold him tight and never let him out of her sight again.

She pushed open the door and began to race up the steps toward where she had seen Audrey.

Kevin followed her inside but then took one look outside to make sure they weren't followed. Satisfied that he hadn't seen anything, he closed the front door. While Annie went upstairs to meet their friends, Kevin decided he was going to have a seat and catch his breath. He felt like he had been holding it this whole night. After being chased by the dogs and seeing Henry's body laying lifeless on the ground, Kevin needed to relax a bit, or he was going to have a heart attack.

Kevin sat down at the kitchen table, pushing away a bowl of decaying fruit as far from him as he could get it. He took a deep breath, trying to calm his nerves. In doing so, he got a big whiff of something he really hoped he wouldn't.

It was the smell of death.

Upstairs, Annie had made her way all the way up to the top floor. She made sure not to step in the blood trails of the dead kids who had lived here. It felt like it would be wrong to step where they spent their last moments. Kind of like when you were young, and it felt wrong to step on a crack for fear of breaking your mother's back.

Annie walked over to the door that led to the window where she had seen the figure at. Pushing it open she saw...an empty room.

There was nobody there.

Even Javier's space had been vacated, just like she thought it would. Which meant that they now knew for sure that there was another homicidal ghost on the loose. But she was pretty sure he would be far from here, probably exploring another building and trying to find people to prey on.

But she knew that she had seen somebody up here.

She ran across the hall to the other rooms, checking them one by one. Each room yielded similar results.

Annie began to breathe a little quicker. Her heart began to race. She thought that she might be having a panic attack. She had been so sure that she saw somebody up here. She had gotten her hopes up that she might see her friends. That she would be back in Chuck's arms and that he was going to protect her from all the bad things on this island.

Annie's breathing stopped. She had walked back into the hallway and was about to go back downstairs when she saw something.

There was a child walking in front of her.

Annie remembered Maverick saying that the island tended to remember the awful things that happened here. Was the house remembering what happened to the kids? Were they coming back inside to meet their death? Was that whole horrible, awful scenario about to play out in front of her?

She hoped not. She couldn't bear to see a child get murdered in front of her.

Just then, Kevin called up the stairs.

"Annie?" he said.

Without thinking, she responded.

"Yeah?" Annie managed to croak out.

With that, the child's neck snapped in her direction. Its eyes locked on hers and its arms reached out to her. It began to waddle toward her, arms outstretched. It was as if the child wanted to be picked up, to be held one more time.

Annie's insides broke down. Her mind went back to the day when she had lost her own child. She had had a stillborn baby. She and Chuck had been devastated and she had never gotten over the loss of her would-be child. To be able to carry it to full term and not be able to carry it in real life had weighed on her mind every day since.

As the child in front of her reached out its arms, she couldn't help but reach back.

Bending down, Annie grabbed the child under the arms and lifted it, swaddling the child as close to her as she could. As if on instinct, she leaned in and sniffed the top of the child's head.

She instantly pulled her head back in disgust.

The baby smelled like death.

Annie extended her arms, putting the child in front of her. Just then, she remembered where she had seen this child before.

It wasn't one of the Graystone children.

This was the child of Bertha.

Chapter Thirty-Five

Just then, an overwhelming smell pervaded the room. It was the smell of decay, the smell of rotting meat.

Annie looked up just in time to see Bertha step into the hall.

Bertha. The ghost that was overly protective of her child.

The child that Annie was currently holding to her chest.

Bertha's eyes moved from Annie to the child and back. And those eyes filled with an unhuman amount of rage. The kind of rage that would only end when one of the people in this room was killed.

And since Bertha and the child were already dead, that only left Annie.

Annie quickly put the little boy back down, but it was already too late for her.

Bertha began to storm toward her. Annie looked around, but there was no place to run, nowhere to hide.

Downstairs, Kevin had smelled the ghosts from the infirmary. It wasn't a smell he would soon forget. He knew that they had to be around here somewhere, but he wasn't looking forward to finding out where.

Kevin knew that he had to get Annie out of there fast. He walked slowly over to the bottom stairs and called her name. When she answered back, he could sense the fear in her voice.

Just like that, he knew it was too late. The ghosts were already upstairs with her. He struggled with what to do next. He began to inch his way up the stairs, taking deep breaths as he did so.

Kevin tried to talk himself up, to convince his body to move forward. But it didn't want to. He wanted to say Annie's name once more, to confirm if she was alright or not. But he knew that if she was alright, she would come down the stairs eventually. But if she wasn't alright, and there was a ghost upstairs, then calling her name may only trigger that ghost to come after him next.

As much as he tried to convince his mind to let him walk upstairs, he couldn't do it. He was just too afraid.

Kevin mouthed a silent apology to Annie and then quietly tiptoed down the few steps he had climbed back to the main floor.

There he stood, listening for any sounds of Annie or his friends.

Or any sounds of ghosts.

He thought he heard feet pounding upstairs. Were there people running? Then he thought he heard a scream, but it was hard to decipher sounds from downstairs while a storm was raging outside.

He was about to strike up the courage to make another attempt to go upstairs when something happened that he would never forget for as long as he lived.

There was a loud bang, and then pieces of wood splintered down around him.

Kevin shielded his face from the debris that rained down around him. He thought that the ceiling above him must have collapsed under the weight of the fresh rain or maybe it was just old age catching up to it.

He was wrong.

He was horribly wrong.

As the dust settled around him, he brought his arms down from around his face so he could investigate what happened.

Welcome To Nightmare Island

What he saw terrified him to his very core.

There was a hole in the ceiling above him. From it protruded Annie's head.

Blood poured down her face and dripped onto the floor in front of him. Her mouth was agape as she struggled to take one final breath. Annie's eyes met Kevin's, and she slowly mouthed his name before her eyes rolled back and she was silenced forever.

Chapter Thirty-Six

Jonah was running through a dark hallway. After being separated from his friends, he ran into the first building he could find. That building happened to be the asylum. He rounded one corner, feeling lost, trying to find a sign on a wall or any landmark that would tell him that he wasn't just running in circles.

He came to a dead end. Then heard a noise behind him.

Jonah swirled around, expecting to see one of the ghosts there.

Would it be Bertha? Jones Jepsen? The Huntsman and his hounds? Jonah struggled with whether he wanted to find out what the noise was.

It was dark in the hallway, so he couldn't see what had made the noise. He didn't smell the stench of rotting flesh, which meant he probably wasn't near a ghost.

He took a deep breath, steadying himself before proceeding. He hadn't heard anything in a while. Maybe he had just imagined the noise.

After what felt like an eternity, and after much convincing, Jonah got his feet moving again. He began walking slowly back toward where he had come from, away from the dead end, but also toward the direction from where he had imagined the sound had come from.

Just then, a flash of lightning lit up the hallway.

His breath caught in his throat. He had seen something. There was something in this hallway with him.

He stood there, frozen in his steps, unaware of what to do.

Then, another flash lit up the hallway. He could make out a female shape at the end of the hall.

He breathed out a sigh of relief and began to walk toward the figure.

"Audrey, I've been looking all over for you. Where have you been?" He said as he approached the figure in the darkness.

He was almost to the spot where he had seen Audrey's outline in the darkness when the hallway was lit up once more by another flash of lightning.

Jonah froze once more.

The feminine figure did not belong to Audrey.

It belonged to Mabel.

And she was right in front of him.

Chapter Thirty-Seven

Jonah could feel a scream welling up in his throat as he looked into the eyes of the beautiful ghost. He could feel it, but it didn't want to come out. Jonah shut his eyes. He didn't know how her power worked; Miles hadn't gotten around to explaining very well how she did her thing.

He stood in the hallway, eyes closed, holding his breath, waiting for death's sweet release.

But nothing happened.

He stole up enough courage to open one eye and was astounded by what he saw.

Jonah wasn't in the asylum anymore. Or at least, not the asylum that he was used to seeing.

This one was brightly lit. The tiled floors gleamed with fresh wax. It all seemed very sanitary to him like a normal hospital would be.

Jonah looked around, expecting to see Mabel nearby, but she was nowhere to be seen.

This was weird. Had he fallen and hit his head? He could have sworn that it was dark out before, but through the window, at the end of the hall, he could see sunlight pouring in.

And the brightness in this hallway, what a complete change from what he was used to experiencing in this asylum. Even when the group of friends had toured the asylum with Miles, it had been extremely dark in the halls of the old building.

He had to have hit his head or something. He must have fallen and woken up during the day after the tour had ended and everyone went home, and someone had turned the lights back on.

The tour!

He had completely forgotten about it. If the sun was out, then he must be late for the boat. His friends wouldn't leave without him, would they?

He ran to the window, hoping to catch a glimpse of the dock in the distance. Craning his neck, he could almost see it from this angle, but his eyes stopped on something else.

The courtyard out front had completely changed overnight. Gone were the overgrown landscaping and the hedges that seemed to reach for the heavens. Instead, everything was trimmed properly, with not a blade of grass out of place. The cobblestone walkways were no longer pitted with potholes deep enough to break ankles.

He could see several of the buildings they had walked through over the past several nights. No longer were the windows broken, the siding in disrepair, and the vines threatening to overtake the buildings and bring them back to the earth.

The buildings now seemed almost new.

Something moving out of the corner of his eye caught his attention. Looking down, he saw two people walking on the cobblestones. They were dressed in scrubs, and one was carrying a clipboard.

There weren't supposed to be any other people on the island.

Maybe it was all a ruse made up to scare people on the tour. But the tour was over, and he needed to get off the island. Back to his friends. Back home, as far away from this place as he could get.

Jonah began to bang on the window, trying to get the attention of the people on the ground below him. "Hey! Up here! I need help!" Jonah yelled.

The nurses stopped in their tracks, looking up at him in shock.

"I need help getting off the island!" He shouted through the glass. "I'm not supposed to be here. I think the boat left without me!"

Suddenly, a door opened behind him.

Jonah swung around in time to see a different pair of nurses come out to greet him.

"Am I glad to see you guys," Jonah said as they approached. "I need help getting off the island," he repeated.

"Well, you're not going anywhere soon," the first nurse said as she caught up with him.

"What?" Jonah asked. "What do you mean?

"How did you get out of your room?" the second nurse asked. This one, a man, grabbed Jonah's arm with a firm grip and began pulling him down the hall.

"What room?" Jonah asked, struggling against the grip of the male nurse. "The hotel room? I walked out of it last night."

The nurses chuckled to each other. "The hotel room, ha! Is that what they're calling it these days? I'll be sure to have the front desk send up your room service when it's ready," the first nurse said.

Jonah didn't understand why these people were being so rude, he just wanted to get back to his friends.

"Look, I don't know what's going on here. All I know is, there was a boat that was supposed to come here at sunrise, and my friends and I were supposed to be on it. I must have woken up too late and missed the boat." Jonah said. "Can you guys call somebody and get me a ride off this godforsaken island?"

"Wish I could buddy, but unfortunately we're not supposed to allow patients out of their rooms unless they are specifically authorized," the male nurse said.

"What patient?" Jonah asked. "I'm not a patient here. I'm a tourist. I was invited here."

Welcome To Nightmare Island

"That's quite the outfit for a tourist," the first nurse said, pointing at Jonah's chest.

Jonah looked down, expecting to see his jacket, but instead, he was wearing a gown.

When did I end up in this? Jonah thought to himself.

"What happened to my clothes?" Jonah asked, freaking out.

"They were taken and put in a storage locker when you were checked into the asylum. You'll get them back when you leave. Though most people don't leave this place." The male nurse said grinning at the other nurse.

Chapter Thirty-Eight

Jonah paced back and forth, his bare feet touching the cold tile. The nurses had grabbed him and put him into a room with padded walls. There was a cot in the corner, but the room was otherwise bare of any furniture.

This had to be an elaborate part of the experience of being on the island. It was the only way that this made sense in his mind. There must be some type of movie magic crew behind all this that could turn around a set in an hour and make it look completely new. Everything around him was probably fake.

Jonah went over to the wall, pulling on the pads meant to protect a patient from harming themselves.

It wasn't budging.

This stuff is on there tight, Jonah thought to himself.

Looking down at his ridiculous gown, he couldn't imagine how they got this onto him. The last thing that he could remember was that it was raining outside, and he was wearing a jacket and pants and...

That was it. He racked his brain but couldn't remember anything that he was doing yesterday. He tried and tried but for the life of him, he just couldn't recall why he was here in the first place. All he knew was that he wasn't supposed to be here.

I must get out of here, Jonah thought to himself.

He walked over to the door, grabbing the handle. It didn't budge. He was locked in this room.

Jonah pressed his face against the glass, hoping to see anyone in the hallway, but there was nobody there.

The two nurses who had brought him there had left.

"HELP!" Jonah shouted at the top of his lungs. "I NEED TO GET OUT OF HERE!"

No response.

He tried again. "HELP!"

"Will you shut the hell up?" someone in the next room said. "You're gonna rile up the other patients."

Jonah didn't know if that was another patient or a nurse. Hell, it could've been a janitor, he was just happy he wasn't left alone here.

"Please, you must help me! I'm not supposed to be here!" Jonah shouted to the man in the other room.

"Yeah, me either. And neither are the rest of the bozos in this building," the man said.

Just then, Jonah could make out a noise coming from a different room in the hall. Several noises.

"Now you've done it," The man said. "You've woken up the rest of the crazies."

Jonah could make out several voices in the hall, rising in volume. It was as if they were triggered by sound, and the louder the noise in the hall got, the louder the people in each room became. It reminded Jonah of two children trying to be heard, each growing louder and louder, speaking over the other until a screaming match broke out.

Those must be the other patients in the asylum, Jonah thought.

As he listened, he could make out a voice yelling, "Help me, help me!" Another was moaning hysterically, and yet another patient was screaming at the top of their lungs, piercing the air with a shrillness that made Jonah cover his ears with his hands.

Devin Cabrera

The noise of it all made Jonah step back from the door. Then he really took in his surroundings.

The padding on the door to his room was ripped and cracked, and torn in several places as if patients had tried to claw their way out of the room. But the more he looked, the more concerned he became.

While the padding on the door was clawed as if someone were trying to get out, there were grooves in the frame, like patients had held on for dear life to prevent them from leaving the room. The grooves in the frame stretched into the hallway, past where the door now stood shut. In one groove, Jonah could see the edge of a fingernail still stuck in the wood.

Why would someone be afraid to leave the room?

He wouldn't have to wait long to find out.

Chapter Thirty-Nine

There came a noise from the end of the hall. A door had opened.

Jonah was surprised that he could have heard a door opening with all the racket going on in the hallway. Then he realized why he heard it.

It was like someone had flipped a switch. The hallway had gone deathly silent. As if all the patients knew that what was coming wouldn't be good. Each one paled into the background, trying to hide the fact that they existed.

But Jonah was new here. He didn't know any better.

Jonah ran to the window to see who it was.

He could hear their footsteps grow louder and louder as the person made their way down the hall toward him.

Finally, the person came into view.

It was the male nurse carrying a clipboard.

A somewhat familiar face, Jonah thought. He began banging on the glass trying to get the nurse's attention.

"Let me out! I'm not supposed to be here!" Jonah shouted through the glass.

The nurse stopped short in front of Jonah's door, looking up to meet his gaze. "It looks like it's your lucky day," the nurse said.

The man opened Jonah's door with one hand, and Jonah could hear the buzz of the electromagnetic handle go off as it swung open. The nurse took one step inside and in one fluid motion, he pulled a needle out of his pocket and jammed it into the side of Jonah's arm.

"What the...ow! That hurt!" Jonah exclaimed. "Why did you do that?"

He was going to complain some more but suddenly, he began to grow extremely lightheaded. He clutched his arm where the needle had gone in, turning his head to see it. But the motion of turning his head was too much for him to handle and it send him spiraling onto the ground.

The last thing he saw was the nurse bent over him with the clipboard before he blacked out completely.

Chapter Forty

The light was so blinding that Jonah thought he might have died.
    Opening his eyes, he realized that he was in a doctor's office, though it was like none he had ever seen before.

Jonah was used to seeing doctor's offices decorated with posters about the effects that smoking has on your body, jars filled with cotton balls and tongue depressors, and a blood pressure cuff hanging on the wall.

This was different.

Jonah was in a windowless room. There was a single light above him that was pointed directly into his face and made it hard to see his surroundings, but what he could make out terrified him. To his left, there was a rolling tray filled with sharp metal objects. The few things he recognized were a scalpel, a few needles, and a bone saw.

What the hell are they gonna do with that? Jonah thought to himself.

Just then, he heard a noise from the corner of the room. Jonah struggled to see what it was, but between the light shining directly in his eyes and how dark the rest of the room was, he couldn't seem to make it out.

Jonah tried to sit up to get a better view but found that he couldn't move. His hands and feet were bound to a gurney with leather straps.

"Ahh, the patient awakens." A man's voice said from the darkness.

Jonah heard footsteps hitting the tile floor coming from the direction of the noise he had heard. He squinted his eyes, trying to see the man, but he still couldn't make out anything.

He didn't have to wait very long.

From out of the darkness came a man dressed in blue scrubs. The lower half of his face was covered by a surgeon's mask. The man also wore a cap over his head that was meant to keep hair from falling out onto a patient.

This man seemed like he was dressed for surgery, but why?

Had Jonah suffered from an accident? Was there some part of him that needed to be fixed that he didn't know about?

No, that's silly. Jonah felt perfectly fine. There was absolutely nothing wrong with him except for the fact that he was strapped to the bed like someone who intended to hurt themselves.

"Hello there," the man said. "I don't think I've seen you here before."

The man stepped closer to the light.

Jonah could see that he was holding a clipboard in his hand. He seemed to be examining a sheet of paper on it, looking very concerned.

"Yes, yes. This is very troubling indeed. Let's see if we can get you fixed up," the man said.

"There's nothing wrong with me," Jonah said. "I don't need to be fixed up. I'm perfectly fine. I'm not even supposed to be here."

The man *tsk-tsked* in disappointment. He placed the clipboard down on the gurney next to Jonah. "A stubborn one, aren't we?" the man said.

Welcome To Nightmare Island

Jonah looked down at the clipboard. The sheet of paper on top was completely bare of anything. There wasn't a list of things wrong with Jonah at all.

"My name is Dr. Stevens. But you can call me the doctor. Most do." The doctor turned and began rummaging through some drawers. "Today we're going to be running some tests on you." The doctor seemed to find what he was looking for. He turned around and walked back over to where Jonah lay helpless.

"What kind of tests?" Jonah said. Or at least, that's what he was trying to say before the doctor pulled something out from behind his back and brought it to Jonah's foot.

He heard a buzzing sound and was immediately met with the most pain he had ever experienced in his life.

The doctor had tased Jonah's bare feet, the shock of which sent a pain through Jonah so bad that he arched his back, protesting the restraints which held him down.

"Ahhhh. What are you. Ah, why?" Jonah tried to scream, but the pain made it hard for him to create full sentences.

Finally, the doctor turned the taser off, picked up the clipboard, and made a few marks.

"Reaction to pain...normal," the doctor muttered under his breath.

"Why the hell did you do that?" Jonah screamed at the doctor.

"To make sure that you had normal pain tolerance levels," the doctor said nonchalantly.

Jonah watched as the doctor went back to the drawer and dropped the taser inside. He took a deep breath. Jonah was glad to see that thing go.

But what he heard next made him wish the taser was back.

Chapter Forty-One

From where the doctor stood on the other side of the room, Jonah could hear a high-pitched whirring noise.

Jonah's skin became covered in gooseflesh.

What the hell was that? What could the doctor possibly pull from his bag of tricks now?

Jonah didn't want to find out, but he was strapped in any-way. There was no place for him to go.

The doctor turned back around, and he began to walk slowly back toward Jonah. As he came into the light, Jonah could see the light reflecting off something in his hands.

It was an electric bone saw.

Jonah began to squirm around on the gurney, trying desperately to free himself. But to no avail.

With each passing moment, the doctor came closer and closer to him. From here, Jonah could already see the gleam in the doctor's eyes.

The eyes were the only part of the doctor's face that Jonah could see. And in those eyes, he could see that the doctor was enjoying this.

He enjoyed seeing Jonah squirm.

He enjoyed causing pain.

Jonah was beginning to wonder if this man was even a doctor at all, or if he was one of the patients. Any man who took pleasure in doing something like this had to be crazy.

The doctor was only a foot away from the bed now, and Jonah's flailing seemed to not be doing him any good. He took a breath, feeling defeated.

"Good, you've calmed down," the doctor said. "Now hold still."

Chapter Forty-Two

The doctor pressed the trigger on the bone saw, making a high-pitched whirring sound. Satisfied that it was working to his liking, he began to move the saw slowly toward Jonah's exposed kneecap.

Jonah began to freak out once more, shifting every free muscle he could.

"Stop moving, or I may accidentally cut off something extra," the doctor said.

Jonah stopped. He closed his eyes, holding his breath as he waited for the doctor to cut his leg off.

The blade was so close to his kneecap that Jonah could feel the breeze from its spinning move his leg hairs.

Just then, a piercing sound filled the room, followed by a bright red light.

Jonah's eyes were closed, but he was pretty sure that the sound was his screaming, and the red was his blood flying across the room. But when he opened his eyes, he saw something that shocked him.

The doctor had straightened up, looking toward the door.

Welcome To Nightmare Island

A bright red light above the door was flashing on and off as an alarm blared throughout the room.

The doctor put the saw down and ran to the door.

As Jonah watched, the door buzzed open and the man raced outside, the door buzzing shut behind him as the electromagnetic locks engaged.

Jonah felt all the air rush back into his lungs. It felt like he had been holding it for hours. He couldn't believe how close he had come to having his leg amputated.

The siren continued to blare, making it hard for Jonah to think. But he knew one thing.

He had to get out of here before that doctor came back.

Jonah shifted both arms, and then his legs, trying to find a weak spot in the leather cuffs that he might be able to squeeze through. But there was nothing.

He tried to slide his hands through the cuffs, but his thumbs kept him from tugging them out all the way.

Just then, he remembered a trick that Chuck had told him that some criminals used to get out of handcuffs.

Jonah shivered. He didn't know if he could do that. The ones that had accomplished it in Chuck's stories were deranged, usually high out of their minds, and virtually unable to feel pain.

But what were his other alternatives? Stay here and wait for the doctor to come back and cut off his legs?

No. He was going to have to do this.

Jonah decided his left hand was going to have to do.

He shifted his body down on the bed, pushing the leather strap as far up his arm as he could, freeing his hand to create as much movement as possible.

Then, closing his eyes, Jonah lifted his hand as high as he could and brought it down thumb first on the railing of the bed.

Jonah screamed, but he hadn't accomplished his goal yet.

He repeated the movement several times, slamming his thumb against the bar until finally, he heard a pop.

Jonah had dislocated his thumb on his left hand.

He opened his eyes. His thumb looked slightly mangled, and he didn't want to look at it for too long for fear that he was going to be sick.

Jonah slid his arm back through the cuff, gingerly sliding it over his now dislocated thumb. After a few seconds of pain, Jonah was able to slide his damaged hand through the cuff.

He let out a deep breath. Trying not to rely on his thumb too much, he reached over and undid the bindings on his other arm, and then moved on to free his legs.

Just then, the light in the room went dark.

The flashing red light had turned off as well. And the piercing siren that had rung overhead had died off completely.

Jonah struggled to see where he was going, trying to remember the shape of the room.

As he did so, he forgot about the tray that was next to the bed, and he smacked his knee on the cold steel support.

Cursing to himself, Jonah managed to find a wall. Feeling his way around the wall, he was able to locate the door.

There's no way the doctor would have left the door unlocked, would he?

Jonah reached for the handle and pulled.

The door clicked and came free.

The locks were on an electromagnetic system. So, when the power had gone out, that meant that the locks were no longer functional.

Lucky me, Jonah thought. But then he stopped, a terrifying thought crossing his mind.

If the locks on his door had become useless, then it was not hard to believe that every lock in the building was now rendered useless.

Including the locks on the rest of the patient's doors.

Chapter Forty-Three

Jonah poked his head through the open door, seeing if the coast was clear.

There was nobody in sight. However, in the distance, he could hear the wails of many people. Their screams echoed down the hall, causing the hair on Jonah's neck to stand on end.

Jonah made his way down the hall, his bare feet slapping the cold tile below. Anytime he heard a noise, he stopped in his tracks. He didn't have a plan of what to do if somebody saw him. He wasn't exactly armed and didn't have any place to hide a weapon in this hospital gown.

Jonah was beginning to regret not picking up one of the tools out of that room to use as a weapon.

Suddenly, he heard footsteps coming toward him from the other end of the hall. The hallway was curved, so he couldn't see who was coming, but he could see their shadows on the wall several yards ahead of him. It appeared to be two people.

And they were getting closer.

Quickly, he ducked into a dark empty room nearby. He stood there in the dark with bated breath, waiting as the two men walked past the door, unsuspecting of a man on the run in the room beside them.

They appeared to be in a rush, hopefully not to the room where he was just strapped to a bed. He could use some more time to get away before anyone realized that he was gone.

The moment that he could no longer hear their footsteps, he sprang out from his hiding place and began to walk in the opposite direction that they were going.

It was very dark in the halls now, with the only light coming from a few emergency lights that probably ran on an external generator somewhere.

Jonah wondered what had caused the power outage, and what may have caused the alarms to go off in the first place.

He came to the end of the hallway, where he stopped to peer out of the window. Careful to not be seen, he peeked around one edge of the window. He had to stop and make sure he was seeing properly.

There were many people outside, none of which happened to be looking up at the asylum. In fact, every one of them appeared to be running away from it as fast as they could.

Jonah couldn't help the feeling that he should be doing the same.

He managed to locate a stairwell and took the stairs to the level below. Once there, he opened the door, hoping to find an exit on this floor that may lead out of this place.

Instead, he opened the door to see one of the nurses running straight at him.

Jonah froze, knowing that his stint of freedom was up. The nurse was about to drug him again and have him taken back up to the room with the leather straps. There he would be forced to wait until the doctor came back to run experiments on him.

He knew that he had to do something, to run away, or to fight, or anything besides stand still and wait to be taken into custody.

The nurse was almost to Jonah now.

But his body refused to move.

Just when he thought the nurse was going to grab him, he instead

Welcome To Nightmare Island

flew right past Jonah. He sprinted past Jonah so quickly that it stirred up a breeze, causing Jonah's hospital gown to flutter in its wake.

Jonah couldn't understand. Why would the nurse run past him? Why wasn't he taken back into custody? Where was he running to?

The better question was, what was he running from?

Jonah was about to find out.

As Jonah made his way down the hall, he became aware of a large commotion up ahead. He proceeded forward with caution. Finally, he rounded the corner and saw what the nurse had been running from.

Chapter Forty-Four

The hallway that had contained the padded room he had been locked up in earlier was now filled with people. There was a mix of patients in gowns and nurses in scrubs. The dull, sterile environment of the asylum hallway had recently acquired a new color palette.

The walls and floors were now coated in blood.

It appeared that once the power had gone out, the patients had realized that the locks on their doors were no longer working and had escaped their rooms. Knowing that there was likely no way for them to escape from the island, they decided to turn their attention to their captors. There were not enough nurses on staff to contain the flux of patients that were now streaming through the halls, and those who hadn't had the foresight to run out of the building were now being dragged through the halls like playthings.

Jonah watched as two particularly big patients seemed to be playing a game of tug of war, and they were using one of the nurses as a rope.

Unfortunately for the nurse, he was awake for all of this.

Jonah listened as the man screamed for help from his colleagues, all of which seemed busy dealing with their own problems. Jonah watched in horror as the man's arms were pulled out of their sockets, ripping the nerves and tendons under his skin.

Other nurses weren't so lucky. Some of them appeared to lie dead in the halls, their skulls having been smashed to a pulp against the walls.

One patient sat on top of a fallen nurse. He had managed to wrestle a syringe from the man and had begun to stab the nurse repeatedly with the needle end. The nurse's shirt had begun to sprout hundreds of little pinpricks of blood. His body convulsed as blood spewed out of his mouth and down the sides of his face.

Jonah didn't know how long he was standing still, but it was long enough that one of the patients finished dealing with a nurse and began to walk toward him.

Jonah gawked as the massive man started to pick up speed, getting closer and closer to him. That's when he felt the presence to his left.

Looking around, he saw the nurse that had originally put him in the padded room. The man was reaching up to grab Jonah. But just when he was about to do so, the patient that had been walking toward Jonah grabbed the nurse and threw him against the wall. As the nurse recovered from the throw, the patient stamped on the back of the man's calf as hard as he could.

There was a sickening crunch as the bone underneath snapped in two.

Jonah knew that it was time for him to get the hell out of there.

He ran down the hallway, jumping over the limp bodies of the nurses. His feet were slick with the blood of those around him, and they stuck to the floor with every step. Jonah kept running, no matter what horrible sounds he heard coming from behind him.

Finally, he found the front door.

Jonah had never been so happy to see daylight before. He pushed through the front doors, streaming out into the fresh air, which still smelled like a freshly dug grave. He would never get used to that smell, but it was much better than the coppery smell of blood that filled the hallway he had just left.

Behind him, the front doors blasted open.

Spinning around, he saw that many of the patients had followed him outside, and they were now running off toward the other buildings around the island.

Jonah knew that he had somewhere else to be though. He took off toward the edge of the island, trying to locate where the dock was with the boat that led off this island.

It had been foggy the last time he had seen the boat, so he didn't know exactly where it was. But logic told him that if he followed the coastline, eventually he would run into it.

Looking back, he could see the buildings he was leaving behind. The asylum stood tall and menacing even in the daytime. In the distance, he could see the hotel, and even farther away he could see the infirmary. No doubt they were both currently being overrun by the patients.

He turned forward again. There was nothing he could do about that. The only thing he needed to focus on was finding the boat and getting off this island.

Jonah ran to the coastline, getting closer and closer until he was forced to stop abruptly.

He was standing on the edge of a cliff. The water was lapping at the rocks below, hundreds of feet below where Jonah was standing.

Obviously, the dock wasn't here. He hadn't remembered scaling a cliff when he got here. But from this vantage point, he might be able to see the boat. He squinted his eyes, trying to see the dock anywhere along the coastline.

What he saw made his heart drop.

He saw the boat.

The boat was loaded with people. And it was currently halfway to shore, heading in the opposite direction.

"Hey!" Jonah yelled, trying to get their attention. "Come back! I need to get on that boat!"

Welcome To Nightmare Island

Maybe they didn't hear him, Jonah thought. The wind on most lakes tended to be stronger than on land due to having no resistance. Maybe it was too loud for them to hear anything.

But then, it appeared that the wind had carried his voice all the way to them.

The people on the boat all looked up directly at him. And then they began to row faster.

Why were they ignoring me? Jonah thought.

Then he looked down.

Jonah was currently wearing the outfit of the same people who had just killed their colleagues. He was also barefoot and covered in blood.

Yeah, I probably wouldn't stop for me either, Jonah thought.

Just then, Jonah saw something at the base of the cliff. He couldn't really make it out, it may just have been a trick of the water on his eyes. But he had to make sure he wasn't seeing things. Jonah had to get closer.

He took a few more steps nearer to the edge and leaned over, craning his neck to see.

Just then, he heard a commotion behind him and turned to see the doctor running toward him.

Jonah's eyes grew wide.

Not only because the doctor that had recently tried to cut him open was right behind him, but also because he had just lost his footing.

Jonah's mouth opened in a silent scream as he put his foot down, only to be met with open air. His body plunged downwards, and the last thing he saw was the doctor's face leaning over the edge before he plunged into the freezing cold water below.

Chapter Forty-Five

That's when Jonah woke up.

It was pitch black where he was. He reached around, feeling until he found a flashlight.

Turning it on, he realized that he was back in the asylum, except it was nighttime again. He felt for his thumb which had been dislocated. Thankfully, it was back to normal. It was all a dream. A really, really messed up dream.

And unlike when he normally woke up from a dream in his cozy, warm bed, he woke up from a dream only to be met with a nightmare.

He was still on the island. He was still in the asylum. And there were homicidal ghosts roaming the island trying to kill him.

That's when he remembered what happened. The last time he was here, he had run into Mabel, the ghost that had the power to make you believe you were somewhere else entirely.

She must have used her messed up ghost powers to make me dream that I was here in the past, Jonah thought.

He shuddered, thinking back to what he had just lived through. They did some really messed up stuff to the patients in this place, and he had almost become one of the victims of the asylum.

Welcome To Nightmare Island

There's still time for that, Jonah thought to himself. He tried to push that thought away. One thing he knew for sure though was that he needed to get out of the asylum.

He got up and began to run down the hallway, flashlight leading the way. At one point he stopped, trying to figure out where he was. He tried to remember how the place looked like in the daytime during the dream that Mabel had put him through.

It was while he was doing this that he heard a noise coming from somewhere down the hall.

Jonah froze, unable to breathe. Trying not to be heard by whatever evil thing was lurking around the next corner. He was able to identify the sounds of footsteps, and they were getting louder.

Whatever it was, it was coming toward him. He couldn't walk away because whatever it was would hear him and chase after him. He also couldn't stand still, because then it would just walk right into him.

No. Jonah had to face whatever it was.

As the footsteps seemed to round the corner, Jonah stepped out, shining his flashlight in the thing's face.

He dropped his flashlight in surprise.

It was Audrey.

"Audrey!" Jonah said, rushing over to hug his girlfriend. It felt like it had been days since he saw her, and all his worries for Audrey's safety came flooding back.

She squeezed him back briefly, but then quickly pulled away.

Jonah was confused. Was she not excited to see him?

He looked at Audrey's face, only to realize that there was a look of sheer terror upon it.

"What's wrong?" Jonah asked.

"It's Chuck," Audrey said. "His mind has been taken over by Javier. He's trying to kill me."

Just then, Jonah heard another set of steps coming down the hall.

He looked past Audrey's shoulder, just in time to see Chuck coming down the hall.

There was something odd about him. Something Jonah had never seen before. Chuck seemed off. His head was tilted down as he walked, and he looked up at Audrey and Jonah with pitch-black eyes that didn't have a trace of white in them.

Catching sight of them, Chuck stopped. His mouth turned up into an evil smile that didn't reach his eyes.

Jonah caught a glimmer in Chuck's hand as something reflected the light of the flashlight. As his eyes focused on the object, he realized it was a scalpel.

Audrey turned, seeing Chuck behind her.

"Run!" Audrey shouted, turning back to Jonah, and pushing him down the hall.

Chuck seemed to take this as his cue to move. He began to lumber after them, scalpel in hand. The whole time that wicked grin seemed to get bigger and bigger.

"What the hell is wrong with him?" Jonah shouted to Audrey up ahead.

"Javier did something to him. Made him believe that we are the enemy or something," Audrey said. "Whatever is chasing us, it's not Chuck."

They made several turns in the dark, moving through many rooms in the asylum that they had never seen before. All the while, they could hear Chuck's footsteps ever present behind them. Suddenly, Audrey came to a stop in front of Jonah, her flashlight searching the wall in front of them. There was no door here, and no windows either. It was just a blank wall.

A dead end.

They turned around to see Chuck standing there. He was blocking the way out and seemed to understand that his victims were trapped. He was going to take his time with this, like a cat playing with its food.

"You don't have to do this," Jonah said to his friend. "We are not your enemy."

Chuck didn't respond. He just took a few steps closer.

Welcome To Nightmare Island

Jonah stepped in front of Audrey. If it was the last thing he did, at least he would go down protecting his girl.

Suddenly, Chuck reached out with the scalpel as if to stab Jonah with it.

Jonah had been expecting this, and he parried the blow with his flashlight, knocking the scalpel out of Chuck's hands and sending it clattering across the floor. He then whipped the butt of the flashlight forward, straight into Chuck's nose.

He heard the snap of Chuck's nose breaking, and blood immediately began to gush down his face.

Jonah stepped back, wondering how Chuck would react.

But Chuck didn't even flinch. It was like he was being controlled by someone else who didn't feel Chuck's pain.

Instead of crying out, Chuck lunged forward, wrapping his hands around Jonah's throat, and forcing him backward until his back was against the wall. Then he squeezed, putting so much power into it that Jonah could feel his body lifting against the wall. In no time at all, his feet were dangling above the ground. Chuck's fat fingers stretched around Jonah's throat, blocking off his airways and causing him to fight for breath. He felt like his eyes were going to explode from the pressure.

All that Jonah could do was kick out at Chuck and try to pry his fingers loose. Though try as he might, he received no reaction from Chuck.

Out of nowhere, Jonah saw Audrey run up behind Chuck. In her hand was the scalpel that Jonah had knocked out of Chuck's hands.

She hesitated for only a second, looking up to meet her boyfriend's eyes, before stabbing the blade of the scalpel into the back of Chuck's leg.

This seemed to be the one thing that had got his attention.

Chuck fell to the ground, unable to support Jonah's weight as well as his own on a bad leg.

Audrey must have hit an important nerve or something, Jonah

thought. On one hand, he hoped that his friend was okay. On the other hand, he was glad to be free from Chuck's grasp.

Jonah crawled away from Chuck, choking as he held his own throat and struggled to breathe fast enough to make up for his lost supply of air.

Audrey ran over to Jonah, making sure that he was okay. Once she was sure he was able to breathe again, she pulled him to his feet.

"Come on, we have to get out of here," Audrey said.

Together, they ran off into the darkness.

Behind them, Chuck reached back and pulled the scalpel out of his leg. Blood poured down his calf, soaking his previously white sock. Then he got back to his feet, limping a few steps before figuring out how to transfer his weight properly with one bad leg.

Then he staggered off after his friends.

Jonah and Audrey made their way through the endless corridor. They came to a point where it branched off in every direction.

Jonah paused, trying to remember where they were. Had he been here in his dream?

In the distance, they could hear Chuck limping toward them.

"This way!" Jonah shouted, letting his flashlight guide them. They came upon a hallway that looked familiar, and Jonah picked up his pace.

They could see the end of the hall now. The glass window of the front door lit up as a bolt of lightning flashed across the sky.

Jonah and Audrey burst through the doors, taking in a breath of air, and feeling the rain on their skin. It was like a starving man finding food. They rejoiced in their freedom from the halls of the asylum.

They had forgotten one crucial thing though.

Chuck.

They looked back at the front door to the asylum.

Standing there on the other side of the door, looking through the glass right at them, was Chuck. His pitch-black eyes seemed to stare into their souls. His chest rose and down as his breathing came out ragged.

The evil grin was gone from his face.

Chuck now wore a face of utmost rage.

Jonah had never seen his friend this angry. Chuck had used his police training to keep his composure even during the most stressful situations. This was new territory for him.

Unless he was expressing Javier's feelings right now.

But Javier wasn't done with the friends quite yet. The body that he had chosen to take over was now weak and unable to capture the other people on the island.

If he couldn't cause them bodily pain, he would have to cause them a different kind of pain.

As his friends watched, Chuck raised the blade of the scalpel to his throat.

"No!" Jonah shouted, running back toward the asylum.

But it was too late.

With a simple flick of his wrist, Chuck dragged the blade across his own throat.

Jonah had gotten to the door just in time to see Chuck's eyes turn from black to blue again. He saw the recognition in his eyes. The recognition of what he was doing.

Chuck dropped the scalpel, placing his hands on his throat to stop the blood, which poured through the gaps in his fingers just the same.

Jonah had to help his friend, he couldn't just stand here and watch Chuck die.

He tugged on the door handle, but it didn't budge. Javier had made Chuck lock the door from the inside just before he made him take his own life.

And now Javier was making Jonah watch as his friend died in front of him.

Chapter Forty-Six

Jonah stood on the front steps of the asylum. He had spent the last several minutes pounding on the glass, crying out to his dying friend. But he knew it was too late. He had tried everything to get to Chuck. Hitting the glass wasn't working, so he found a rock and threw it as hard as he could against the glass, but to no avail. The windows in this place were reinforced to keep people in.

Jonah watched as the light faded from his friends' eyes, before sinking to the steps below. He was too pissed off and saddened to think.

Finally, Audrey had to pull him away from his thoughts.

"Come on, we have to get out of here," Audrey said. "It's too late for Chuck, but we have other friends on this island that need our help. It might not be too late for them."

Jonah didn't want to leave his friend's side, but he knew it was what he had to do.

He stood up, pressing his hand against the glass once more, and silently said goodbye to his friend.

Then he turned and walked into the night.

Audrey followed him, as they both went off to look for their friends.

Where would they go? Audrey thought. What was safe? Where could their friends possibly hide to get away from the murderous ghosts outside?

That's when she remembered the Huntsman and his hounds. Were they still outside? Roaming the grounds, searching for a corpse to chew on?

They already had one dead friend; she didn't want to think of having another one. Audrey quickened her pace.

Eventually, a building began to loom out of the darkness. As they grew closer, they realized it was the library. The former home of the ghost Mabel, who Jonah had the misfortune of running into earlier in the asylum.

They hesitated before going into the building. They didn't know what ghosts may be inside. But if Mabel had been in the asylum, hopefully, this one was clear.

Maybe they would even run into the rest of their friends inside.

That made Audrey's heart fill with dread.

Normally, she would have been excited to see her friends. But now, if she were to run into Annie, she would be forced to tell her about Chuck.

Audrey had already seen Jonah's reaction, and that had absolutely devastated her. And Chuck was only Jonah's best friend. Annie was Chuck's girlfriend. They were intimate together, likely planning on spending their lives together side by side for eternity.

But that was over now. Annie would never see Chuck again.

They decided they would go for it.

Taking a deep breath, they pushed open the doors to the library and walked through.

The couple was instantly greeted by the smell of leather-bound pages. Dust motes filtered through their beams of light as they shone their flashlights throughout the room.

They knew that Mabel wasn't here, but they didn't know if any of the other ghosts had taken up refuge in the library. Unfortunately for them, the library shelves created a maze that could hide anyone or anything inside of it.

Jonah decided to check around one of the shelves, and he motioned toward another one for Audrey to check. She nodded, understanding the need to split up and cover more ground.

Jonah covered the beam of his flashlight. Just in case there was something on the other side of this shelf, he didn't want to give away the fact that he was here in case the ghosts didn't already know. He put his back to the end of the shelf, stepping carefully so as to not make a sound. He edged his way closer to the other side, then with a deep breath, he spun out onto the other side of the shelf, shining his flashlight to reveal... an area void of human life.

There was nobody there. It was just a reading nook with a few chairs and a coffee table set up. On the coffee table, there was a stack of bookmarks long forgotten.

Just then, Jonah heard a sound that made his blood run cold.

"Oh my god!" Audrey shouted.

Jonah almost dropped his flashlight. The disruption to the eerie silence made his heart feel like it was going to beat out of his chest.

Had Audrey found a ghost? Did he send her to her death? Was she okay?

These were the questions that were running through Jonah's mind as he raced to where Audrey had been. Only that now, in his rattled state, he couldn't figure out where that was. Every shelf seemed to look the same to him. Did she go behind the shelf with the leather tomes or the shelf with the paperbacks?

Jonah could feel his heart beating faster. It became harder for him to breathe. Was he having a panic attack?

"Jonah!" Audrey yelled.

This snapped Jonah out of it. He followed the sound of Audrey's voice to a dark corner of the library. Once there, he found Audrey facing someone on the ground.

Welcome To Nightmare Island

Not a ghost.
It was Kevin.

Chapter Forty-Seven

Jonah shined his flashlight on his friend.

Kevin was curled up in a ball. He was clutching his knees to his chest and was rocking back and forth. Tears streamed down his face and soaked his shirt, which Jonah could see now was also soaked in blood.

Jonah raced to his friend's side.

"Are you alright?" Jonah asked. "What happened? Why are you covered in blood?"

He had so many questions, but Kevin didn't seem ready to answer any of them. He was still rocking back and forth, and his eyes didn't seem to register that his friends were even there. Kevin was lost in his own thoughts, alone in a world of his own.

Audrey reached out and touched Kevin's hand.

Suddenly, he snapped awake from his trance. He jumped up from his place on the floor, moving as if he was going to swing at Audrey.

That's when Jonah stepped in, grabbing his friend, and pushing him against the wall.

Welcome To Nightmare Island

"Calm down!" Jonah said. "It's your friends! It's Jonah and Audrey."

At the sounds of their names, Kevin's eyes seemed to focus. The manic look on his face melted away. Suddenly, his eyes met Jonah's, instantly filling once more with sadness, and Kevin collapsed into his friends' arms.

"She's gone," Kevin cried into Jonah's shoulder.

"What do you mean? Who's gone?" Jonah asked.

"An-a-Annie," Kevin stammered out. "One of the ghosts got to her. By the time I found her, it was too late."

Now it was Audrey's turn to drop to her knees. She began to sob into her hands. Annie was her best friend. They had done everything together ever since they met seven years ago.

And now, that was over.

Jonah looked down at Audrey. He felt that he should comfort her, to tell her that everything was going to be alright.

But it wasn't. Two of their friends had died. They would never see them again.

Jonah felt that maybe he should give Audrey a moment to herself to deal with some of her newfound grief. In the meantime, he felt he had a duty to break the news to Kevin.

"Annie wasn't the only one," Jonah said quietly.

Kevin looked up from behind his tears. Then he searched behind Jonah, looking for the rest of the group. He only saw Audrey.

"Where's Chuck?" Kevin said.

Jonah didn't answer him. Instead, he hung his head low, unable to bring himself to say it.

Kevin grabbed Jonah by the shirt, pulling his face closer to his own. "Where is Chuck?" Kevin repeated.

Taking a deep breath to steady himself, Jonah said, "He didn't make it."

Kevin's face dropped. "What do you mean he didn't make it?"

"Javier got to him. Took over his mind and made him want to kill us. But before he could do so..." Jonah struggled to finish his sentence. "Javier forced Chuck to take his own life."

Kevin released his hold from Jonah's shirt. He stepped backward until his back was up against the wall, and then he slid down it. He felt like everything was spinning, and it would be best if he was standing for this. Two of his friends had died today.

And even worse was the knowledge that they weren't out of the woods yet. All the ghosts were still out there, waiting to stumble upon Kevin and his friends and kill them too. They would roam the island, hunting down him and his friends until there was none of the living left on the island.

"Come on," Jonah said to Kevin and Audrey. "We have to get up and find a way off this island. If not, then our friends would have died in vain. Let's not let their sacrifices be in vain."

"For Chuck and Annie," Kevin said.

Audrey nodded, wiping a tear from her cheek.

Together, they stood up and began to walk through the maze of bookcases.

That's when they heard footsteps coming their way.

Chapter Forty-Eight

Jonah stopped, holding his arms out to either side to prevent his friends from moving forward.

"Did you guys hear that?" Jonah whispered to his friends.

They stood still, listening for the slightest sound of movement.

"I can hear you," a voice whispered back.

Jonah's heart stopped beating in his chest. There was a ghost in the room with them. And it spoke, which meant...

Jones Jepsen had entered the library.

"Come out, come out, wherever you are," Jones Jepsen sang in a sing-song voice that echoed throughout the room.

Suddenly, a resounding crack boomed around the room. Jones had tossed up a book and blasted it across the room with his mallet. The result was a hundred-year-old book exploding apart, casting sheets of aged parchment fluttering down around the friends.

Jonah looked up at the sheets falling around them like snow. It was almost beautiful. It almost made up for the fact that there was a homicidal maniac running loose in the room that they shared.

"We have to get out of here," Jonah whispered to his friends.

"I'm dead, not deaf," Jones Jepsen said. "I can hear your hearts beating. They're getting faster and faster. It's like the ticking of a clock attached to a bomb. Eventually, the ticking will stop, and so will your heart. And when it does, I'll be there to watch."

With that, a thick book on the shelf behind Jonah and his friends fell to the ground.

The friends whipped around, only to see Jones Jepsen sticking his face through the shelf. There was a wicked grin on his face, like this was a game and he was winning.

"Boo," he said with a smile, his eyes lighting up.

"Run!" Jonah shouted, taking off with his friends.

Behind them, they could hear Jones laughing maniacally and giving himself a round of applause. "Let the games begin!" he shouted.

Jonah tore through the shelves of books, with Kevin and Audrey at his heels. This place felt like it went on forever, and there were several times when they had to double back on themselves after finding themselves walled in by books.

On the other side of the room, they could hear Jones Jepsen skipping through the shelves. He had his trusty mallet with him and whenever something got in his way, he would blast it apart.

Jonah and his friends found themselves at another dead end. They were about to turn around and run out when Kevin stopped them.

"I don't hear anything," Kevin said. "Do you think he stopped looking for us?"

In response, Jones swung his mallet at a bookcase, sending it tipping over into another shelving unit. This created a domino effect, as each bookcase fell over one by one.

"What's that sound?" Audrey asked.

The shelves were too tall to see over, but they heard the commotion getting louder.

Kevin couldn't contain himself, he had to see what the noise was. Carefully he stepped on one of the shelves of the bookcase in front of him. Using the top shelf as a handle, he hoisted himself up onto the next shelf until he could see what was happening.

"Oh shit!" Kevin yelled. "The bookcases are falling over!"

And they were headed right for them.

Kevin jumped down to the floor, determining the best route of escape, and decided that finding their way out of the dead end was too risky. It could take too long, and they might get stuck between the falling shelves.

No, they only had one option.

"Come on," Kevin said. "We have to go over the bookcases." He jumped as high as he could, catching on to the top shelf of the bookcase farthest from Jones. He used all his upper body strength to pull himself up in one go. Once he was on top of the bookcase, he tested it out, hopping up and down slightly to test his weight. These shelves may be hundreds of years old, but they were built to hold some serious weight. Which made sense, since leather-bound books weren't exactly light.

He looked out across the library, seeing the shelving dominoes growing closer. And at the other end, where the shelves had already fallen, he could see Jones Jepsen.

Jones was staring right at Kevin, a huge grin on his face. He then pointed at Kevin like he was Babe Ruth calling his shot. He got into a batter's position and then swung the mallet through the air like a bat. He began to laugh maniacally once more.

Kevin knew they needed to get the hell out of this place. He reached down, giving Audrey a hand up. Jonah followed shortly after.

Just then, the shelving unit in the aisle behind them began to tilt toward the friends.

They had to go. Now.

Jonah led the way, jumping from the top of one shelf to another, only looking back long enough to see if his friends were following him.

They were.

And so was Jones Jepsen.

Because he had knocked down all the shelves, he no longer had to search each corner and cubby for them. He could see exactly where they were always. He stepped from one fallen case to another, squashing the occasional rare book and first edition that had previously been preserved forever in time.

Jones Jepsen was gaining on them, one step at a time. And Jonah could already see the end of the bookcases. Soon, there would be nowhere to jump to. He searched the area, looking for one last option. An exit or a back door of sorts.

Then he saw it.

There was a door right at the end of the last bookcase. Did it lead outside?

Jonah hoped so. Otherwise, they would probably get squished by books or by the mallet of a madman.

He pointed it out to his friends as he ran. Finally, he reached the last bookcase. He decided to jump, tucking himself into a rolling position as he went to break his fall. It was something he had seen in a movie once and had always wanted to try it.

However, it doesn't work very well if you aren't very young or well-practiced.

Jonah rolled but mistimed the fall, and his extra speed sent him into the wall. This didn't feel good, but his adrenaline kept him going. He shot up and helped his friends get down from the top of the case. In the distance they could hear the other shelves falling one by one, getting closer and closer.

And behind that, they could hear Jones Jepsen, whistling as he went. He was literally creating a murder path to them.

They didn't have much time.

Jonah reached for the door handle.

It was locked.

He couldn't handle this right now. This was the only way out. This was their only shot. Without it, they would have to turn and face Jones Jepsen.

Just then, Kevin grabbed a heavy leatherbound book off the shelf. He brought the binding edge of it down upon the door handle, knocking it clean off the door. The old metal infrastructure inside didn't stand up much to brute force.

Kevin dropped the book, pulled the door open, and rushed inside. Jonah and Audrey followed behind, disappearing into the dark room.

Chapter Forty-Nine

They closed the door behind them. Inside was a small room. Jonah shone his flashlight around, hoping to see a backdoor.

But there was none to be seen.

The friends had broken into a storage closet used to house cleaning supplies and extra bookmarks and the like.

Just then, they heard a loud crash from the other side of the door.

Kevin pushed on it.

"It's stuck!" Kevin said.

Jonah joined him. Together they put all their weight against the door, but it wouldn't budge.

The last bookcase must have fallen against the door, trapping them inside.

They heard Jones Jepsen outside the door.

"Come out of your room children, it's time for supper!" Jones yelled through the door, then he cackled at his awful joke.

Jonah spun around with his flashlight, looking for anything that they could use as a weapon. What could you use to defend yourself against a ghost? How could you harm something that was already dead?

He didn't find anything that would do more than give Jones a papercut. But he did see something else. Something better than a weapon.

Jonah pointed his flashlight at the wall above him.

Above one of the shelves was a ventilation shaft that led to the outside wall. It must have been put here to let out any fumes if any of the chemicals from the cleaning supplies spilled. Jonah hoped that the vent would lead outside.

"Help me out with this," Jonah said pointing at the shelf.

Together, he and Kevin moved the shelf away from the wall.

"Give me a boost," Jonah said.

Kevin cupped his hands, providing a place for Jonah to step up.

Jonah climbed up, then holding onto the edge of the grate with one hand, he shone his flashlight through it with the other.

"It leads outside!" Jonah shouted.

He was able to see a hinge at the top of the grate, meaning that they would simply have to lift it up and then crawl through.

Suddenly there came another loud crash against the door. The sudden noise caused Jonah to lose his balance, and he fell to the floor, wincing in pain.

Jones Jepsen had made it to the storage door and was trying to break through. As they watched in horror, the door bounced back slightly as he slammed into it with his mallet. This time, a few splintered pieces came off as the door began to crack.

"We have to go!" Jonah shouted over the noise of another blow from Jones's mallet.

He locked his fingers together, creating a cup with his hands and instructing Kevin to do the same. Then Audrey stepped up, opening the vent grate, and used a boost from both boys to pull herself in.

Bang!

Another crash came from the door, this time creating a hole big enough to see through.

They could see Jones peeking through at them, his grin growing as he could see the fear on their faces.

"You can't hide from me, you know," Jones said. "Sooner or later, I will get you. And then I will rip you apart."

That was all Jonah needed to burst into action. He stepped into Kevin's hands, though with only the help of one person to boost him up, it was a lot harder for him to get inside the vent. His body was tired from all the work it had been put through today and it was taking a toll on him now.

Another crash came at the door, sending a whole plank of wood to the ground.

"Hurry up!" Kevin shouted. "What is taking so long?"

"I'm trying!" Jonah shouted back. Then with one big heave, he mustered what strength he had left and pulled the rest of his body into the vent.

In all their haste, they had made one big miscalculation.

The vent wasn't big enough to turn around in quickly.

And Kevin was the short one of the group.

And there was nobody on the ground to boost him up.

Jonah realized this almost too late.

He couldn't turn around all the way, so he stuck one of his legs out of the vent.

"Grab onto my leg!" Jonah shouted to Kevin.

Kevin did so, jumping as high as he could and grasping onto Jonah's foot.

Jonah didn't have the leg strength to pull Kevin up. He was fit, but there weren't enough leg days at the gym to pull a full-grown man through into a vent with just leg strength alone.

Thankfully, Kevin was able to reach up with his other hand and grasp onto the edge of the vent.

He had just begun to pull himself up when another whack from the mallet sent the door splintering apart.

That's when Jones Jepsen walked into the room.

Welcome To Nightmare Island

Ducking through the hole he had just made in the door, Jones Jepsen looked around the room, observing the small space his victims had just occupied. Then he saw Kevin hanging halfway out of the vent.

Jones cracked his neck from side to side, then went to work.

Chapter Fifty

Kevin's eyes grew wide as he felt a cold dead hand wrap itself around his ankle.

Jones didn't pull at first, just sort of danced his fingers around on the man's skin like spider's legs. He was playing with the man. Jones knew he had won, and now it was time for the fun to begin.

He tugged slightly on Kevin's leg. Not enough to pull him down, but enough to make him feel like he was going to fall to the ground.

Kevin's response was to dig into Jonah's leg with his hand, which he was still holding onto inside the vent.

"Jonah!" Kevin yelled. Jonah tried to turn around, to help in some way, but there wasn't much he could do from inside the vent. He couldn't turn at all with Kevin still grasping onto his leg.

Just then, Jones gave one final tug. A big one. Big enough to rip Kevin's body from the vent and send him sprawling to the floor.

Kevin felt like he was falling for eternity. Before he hit the ground, the last thing he remembered seeing was Jonah's face at the edge of the vent.

Jonah had finally managed to turn around, but it was too late.

Welcome To Nightmare Island

Kevin's body hit the ground with a loud thud, sending up a cloud of dust. The impact of the fall knocked the wind out of him, and he lay there too stunned to move.

Jones walked slowly around Kevin's body. Jonah was reminded of a pack of hyenas circling its prey, trying to scope out a weak area where it could make its move.

Then Jones looked up at Jonah's face staring down from the vent. His wicked grin returned to his face. He brought the end of his mallet up and pointed it at Jonah.

"This one's for you," Jones said with a smile.

Then he brought the end of the mallet down in a wide arc, letting the force of gravity guide the mallet straight into Kevin's skull.

"NO!" Jonah shouted, but it was far too late.

Kevin's head had disconnected from his neck.

Jonah watched as his friend's face bounced off the wall and came back like the sickest game of tennis ever played.

Jones, however, seemed overjoyed.

He swung again, the mallet slamming into Kevin's head once more. There was a solid thunk as it connected. This time, when his head the wall, it didn't bounce back.

"Hahaha! Will you look at all the fun we're having?" Jones said with a laugh. Then he lifted his mallet over his head and began to bring it down repeatedly over all of Kevin's body parts, splintering all his bones and bursting all his organs.

Jonah couldn't watch anymore. He had to get out of this vent. There was no way he was going to let Jones hear him cry. He wouldn't give him that benefit.

Jonah backed out of the vent until he was able to find the exit. Jones's maniacal laughter followed him all the way. Outside, Audrey helped him down to the ground.

"Where's Kevin?" Audrey asked.

Jonah just shook his head, unable to breathe. His hands scrambled all over his body, searching for his inhaler. Finding it, he took two deep puffs. He was finally able to breathe again, but now it felt like his eyesight was going. His vision blurry, Jonah reached up to his eyes, where he found tears streaming down his face.

Audrey's breath caught in her throat. She looked away, far off into the darkness. She bit back tears. Audrey knew what that head shake meant. She wouldn't put Jonah through clarifying it.

Kevin was dead.

It was just her and Jonah now.

Chapter Fifty-One

Jonah and Audrey took a moment to catch their breath.
They had just seen one of their best friends brutally murdered in front of them. Kevin's life had been sacrificed so that his friends could get away.

They wouldn't let his sacrifice be in vain.

The couple had to find a way to get off the island. Or at least find a safe place to hide while they waited for the boat to arrive in the morning.

Just then, Jonah remembered what he had seen at the end of the dream that was forced upon him by Mabel. He leaned in to tell Audrey about it but stopped when he saw a pair of eyes in the darkness in the distance.

"Don't look now, but I think we are being stalked by a ghost," Jonah whispered into Audrey's ear.

Just then, they heard a rumbling growl.

It was one of the Huntsman's hounds.

As Jonah watched, more pairs of eyes popped up in the darkness.

The whole pack was here. Lying in wait for them to show up. And they had arrived.

"Run!" Jonah yelled, pulling Audrey away.

As if they had been called, Jonah could hear the dogs leap into action. Their paws chewed up the mud underneath their claws, sending sprays of dirt into the air behind them.

Thankfully, there was some distance between them and the dogs, and the couple would have a little while to get away from them. Or at least, so they thought.

As they ran, they heard a child crying.

Jonah looked to his left, seeing Bertha and the child. Their clothing was different than when he had last seen them. It appeared to be coated in fresh blood. The blood hadn't had time to dry yet.

With a shudder, he realized that he knew who that blood belonged to. He shook his head, trying to clear it of thoughts of his dead friends. He had one thing to think about right now, get to safety.

Behind them, Bertha and the child altered their course, joining up with the hounds in pursuit of a fresh meal. Apparently, someone had ordered to go.

Jonah and Audrey continued to run through the night. As they passed through the abandoned village that used to house the island's workers, they caught movement out of the corner of their eyes.

Audrey looked around, trying to see what it was.

A flash of lightning lit up the area, and they saw Javier had now joined the group of ghosts chasing after them.

He was too far away for his powers to have any effect on them, but that just gave them more motivation to get as far away as possible from them.

Somehow, all the ghosts that they had met tonight had managed to meet up in the same place on the island for one final hunt.

All except for...

"It's a party now!" Jones Jepsen screamed into the night. He casually skipped across the grounds as he met up with the ghosts. As he skipped, he turned to face the other ghosts. "Long time, no see! Anyone up for a tea party later?"

Javier only glared at Jones.

"No? Too busy now? Maybe we can take a rain check then." Jones howled into the night, laughing at his joke as the rain crashed down around him.

At this point, Jonah could see the edge of the cliff coming up fast. The water at the bottom lit up in the flashes of lightning, showing white caps hurling themselves at the cliff.

Jonah held Audrey back, her skidding feet causing a smattering of rocks to tumble over the edge of the cliff before them. They watched as the rocks fell seemingly forever before finally splashing into the water below. They looked to each other as if seeing if the other had an answer of what to do other than the obvious. They looked back at the ghosts that were chasing them. The ghosts lumbered forward, so close now that they could smell the stench of death that seemed to follow them everywhere they went.

"We have to jump," Jonah said.

Audrey squeezed Jonah's hand. Deep water was her biggest fear, and he knew that. He knew that if she was going to jump, it would take all the courage she had. She wasn't afraid of water; she had learned to swim in summer camp as a young girl. It was what lurked below the surface that scared her. The things you knew were there, that you could feel watching you as you swam. The things that could see you bobbing along on the surface even when you couldn't see them. That is what terrified her.

Jonah gave her hand a squeeze, awakening her from her thoughts of the depths of Lake Sadness. He looked into her eyes, pleading her to have the strength to jump. She knew what she had to do.

"On three, we jump," Jonah said.

Audrey nodded, closing her eyes, and trying not to picture the terrifying things lurking behind and below them.

At this point, the ghosts were so close they could hear them breathing. The hounds ran alongside their master, and the smell of death and decay filled the air as they came ever closer to Jonah and Audrey.

"One," Jonah said as he gave their hands a practice swing. "Two."

"Three!" came a voice from behind them.

Jonah looked back in time to see Jones Jepsen standing over his shoulder.

Without a second thought, Jonah and Audrey leapt off the edge of the cliff. Their hearts felt like they soared into their throats as they dropped.

Jonah's legs dangled in midair as if they were trying to find purchase on the ground below him, but there was nothing but air.

Audrey felt like they were falling for hours. Until suddenly, she opened her eyes, just in time to see the water rushing up toward her, along with the inky darkness it contained.

Their bodies smacked into the water, knocking the wind out of them both. The force of their jump sent them deep underwater.

Jonah kicked and paddled his way to the air above him. So close, but so far away. He kicked and kicked but it never seemed to get closer. Until finally, he broke the surface.

Taking in the deepest breath of his life, he brushed the lake water out of his eyes and looked around him. What he saw made him spin around in circles. Jonah looked in front of him, then behind.

Audrey wasn't there.

"Audrey!" he called out.

Where was she? Had she drowned? She had jumped with him, right?

Jonah looked up toward the top of the cliff. The ghosts that had been chasing him stood at the edge staring down at him.

Then he froze as he felt something tug at his shirt.

Audrey pulled herself out of the water, using his shirt as leverage. She gasped for air, trying to fill her lungs with as much of the stuff as she could.

Jonah took a deep breath. Audrey was alright. He could breathe again. They were far below the reach of the ghosts, and unless the ghosts were able to fly down the cliff then they were gonna be fine.

His relief was short-lived. Jonah felt their bodies sway in the water. The lake water was receding away from the shore as it geared up to send its waves crashing into the rocks at its base.

They were going to have to fight their way to shore or the lake was going to toss their bodies against the rocks like a slab of meat.

Quickly, Jonah scanned the length of the cliff where its base met the water. Most of its sides were too sheer for them to climb up, and even if they did, the waves would hit them and pull them back into the water before they got very far.

Then he saw it.

The thing that Mabel had shown him in the dream.

Chapter Fifty-Two

Off to his right, he saw a dark section of rock that stood out from the rest of the cliff. It was the entrance to a sea cave. Without thinking Jonah said, "Come on, we need to get to that cave!"

They eagerly began swimming toward the entrance, racing the waves to the wall of rock.

Jonah took in gulps of water as he struggled against the waves. He could see the cave entrance getting closer and closer. For a moment he thought they were going to make it.

Jonah glanced back mid-stroke to check on Audrey's progress behind him, and what he saw alarmed him.

A massive wave was approaching right behind her.

He had just a moment to catch his breath before the wave swallowed them both, carrying them forward like a plastic bag in the wind.

Jonah didn't have time to brace himself before he was slammed into the side of the cliff. He felt the air leave his lungs and he saw stars, all the while the waves pulled them back out into the water and prepared to launch them a second time. He barely had time to think before the next wave sent them both crashing against the side again.

This time, however, Jonah was able to get his bearings as they moved.

Just as their bodies were about to hit the wall a third time, he spotted a grooved section nearby.

Then the next wave thrust them into the wall.

Jonah cried out in pain as his ribs took the impact, but in the last second, he reached for the grooves, managing to catch hold with one hand. Once he had a good grip on the stone ledge, he swung his legs around until his feet managed to find purchase as well.

Jonah let in a deep breath. He was back on land.

Then he felt a tug on his leg that almost ripped him off the side of the wall.

Looking down, he saw Audrey holding on to his leg to keep from being dragged back into the water.

Jonah reached down with his free arm and pulled her up, not letting go until she had a firm grip on the rocks herself.

They needed to get to the cave entrance, and fast.

Jonah spotted the dark entrance to the cavern about ten feet from them.

"Follow me!" he shouted over the roar of the waves.

Together, they shimmied their way along the rock wall, finding minuscule grooves to latch their fingertips onto.

They had moved only a few feet when Jonah saw the next big wave coming their way.

"Brace yourself!" Jonah said as he felt the ice-cold water hit him from behind like a ton of bricks. The wave knocked him off balance, and he felt his right shoe lose hold of its grip on the rock face. His feet scrambled to find purchase as his body threatened to plunge back into the water again.

Finally, he felt his shoes catch on the rock, and he could breathe again.

He looked back at Audrey, making sure she was alright before they began their way toward the cave entrance again.

It felt like they had been shimmying along this rockface for hours, even though it had only been a few minutes. Jonah's fingertips felt raw from holding the full force of his weight while grasping the rough edges of the rock.

Finally, they had gotten to the edge of the wall, and he could see the entrance to the cave before him.

The waters of the lake led to a shore made up of boulders, with an opening barely big enough for them to fit through. To enter, they were going to have to jump back into the water and swim inside.

They hesitated, taking a deep breath, before kicking off the side of the wall back into the water.

Jonah would never get used to how cold the water was. If he wasn't killed by ghosts, then he would surely die of hypothermia before the night was up.

They swam inside the cave, pulling themselves up onto the boulders before finally giving themselves a chance to breathe.

They checked each other over, making sure that nothing was broken. Jonah's ribs had been hurt badly when he had been slammed into the rocks, but thankfully they were only bruised. Audrey was fine, though she was shaking like a dope fiend.

Audrey was never one for deep water, but the situation that they were in wasn't helping her fear.

They were both cold, wet, and exhausted.

"It didn't seem like the ghosts could get down here, I think we will be fine for a while. We can probably stay down here until the boat comes, but when it does, we're going to have to swim toward the dock because that boat isn't going to fare well against these rocks. So, we are going to need our energy," Jonah said.

Audrey nodded in agreement. "I'm ju-just so-s-so cold."

"I'll see what I can do about a fire," Jonah said.

Walking around the cave, he managed to find a few pieces of driftwood that were untouched by the storm. Bringing them back to

Welcome To Nightmare Island

where Audrey sat, he dropped the wood and tried to channel everything he learned in the Boy Scouts to this moment. He placed some moss into a pile and began to rub two sticks together until he saw smoke. Seeing a spark, he blew on it until the moss caught fire, then he placed it near the driftwood until the larger piece was fully engulfed.

Jonah had created a fire. His scoutmaster would have been proud. Now, if he could provide enough wood to supply the fire for the next few hours, they could warm up and possibly not get hypothermia.

He took Audrey's hand and pulled her closer to the fire.

They had survived everything up until now, they weren't going to let the cold kill them.

Chapter Fifty-Three

Jonah awoke with a start.

He and Audrey had been so tired that the warmth of the fire had lulled them to sleep.

But now, something seemed off.

Jonah looked around. Audrey was still asleep next to him, but something still didn't feel right. He could still hear the water outside the cavern, but it seemed louder now. The fire must have gone out a while ago, he couldn't even see the embers anymore. It was pitch black inside the cave.

That's when he felt it.

His feet were wet. Not damp from being in the lake earlier, but fully in water.

Jonah grabbed his flashlight, switched it on, and scanned the area around him.

Looking down, he saw that the water level had risen several feet. He couldn't see the embers of the fire because it had been completely submerged.

The water level was rising from the storm, and if they didn't do something quickly, they would both run out of air in this cave.

Welcome To Nightmare Island

"Wake up!" he said as he shook Audrey to life.

She awoke, groggily wiping the sleep from her eyes before remembering where they were.

"The cave is filling up!" Jonah said, pointing at the water quickly rising at their feet.

Audrey jumped up, her eyes scanning the cave. She couldn't see the cave entrance anymore. It had already been completely covered with water.

Being unfamiliar with their surroundings, they wouldn't even know which way to swim to try to find the way out.

The water was pouring in faster now, and they sloshed around in knee-deep water trying to find the exit, but they were unsuccessful.

Audrey, who was still deathly afraid of deep water, was slowly realizing that they were stuck with nowhere to go.

Jonah could see the expressions on her face change as she looked around. The sleepy look she had worn only a few seconds ago was melting away and was quickly being replaced by one of sheer panic.

Jonah had seen this face before, and he knew what he had to do.

He ran over to Audrey's side, grabbing her by the shoulders. "Look me in the eyes," Jonah said. "Breathe. That's it, just breathe. We are going to get out of this."

Audrey took deep gulping breaths as she tried to fight off the oncoming panic attack.

Jonah continued, "We are not going to drown here. The water level can only rise so much and then eventually the air will have nowhere to go. It will create a pocket of air for us to breathe until the water level drops again. We will be fine."

Audrey took another deep breath. She thought about his words for a few seconds, then seeing the logic in his last statement, she began to slowly calm down.

"That's right, deep breaths. We will get through this." Jonah said.

Or at least he hoped they would. Though the air had no place to go, the water continued to rise, and it seemed to be coming in even quicker now.

They waited, listening to the sounds of the water as it continued rising. They held each other, both silently praying that the water would recede, and that they would be able to get out of this cave.

But it didn't.

The water was now shoulder-deep.

Jonah was at the point now where he had to stand on his toes to keep his chin above water.

Audrey on the other hand wasn't so lucky. Being several inches shorter than Jonah, the water had risen past the point of her being able to stand long ago. She was currently being held up in the water by Jonah and could feel her legs already struggling to find purchase on the ground below.

"Why isn't the water stopping?" Audrey asked, her face pointed to the ceiling of the cave.

"I don't know, but we have to keep holding on," Jonah replied. He couldn't make sense of it.

He had attached the flashlight to his belt a few minutes ago. He needed his hands free now to tread water. He needed to find a new solution, and fast, otherwise, they weren't going to make it out of there alive.

They were down to their last inch of air left in the cave. Both were struggling to tread water while also angling their faces toward the cave ceiling to gasp the last remaining bits of air.

Jonah struggled to think between breaths. Theoretically, the water should have stopped coming in when the air had no place to go. So where did the air go?

That's when it came to him. There must be another way out, somewhere above them.

Suddenly Audrey screamed.

"Audrey! Audrey! What's wrong?" Jonah asked.

"I went up for air and something brushed my lips. It felt like it was moving!" Audrey exclaimed.

"What?" Jonah asked. The way she had screamed, he had

thought that a ghost had entered the cave somehow. "Let me turn the light on and we'll see what it is."

He reached for the flashlight, hoping to God that it was waterproof. Flipping the switch to the "on" position, it flickered on. Jonah did a mental fist pump as he pointed the beam toward the direction of the ceiling. His celebration was cut short by what was above him. He had thought there might be a bug on the rock that had grazed Audrey's lips.

What he saw was worse.

Much worse.

Chapter Fifty-Four

Staring back at him were thousands of eyes. Clinging to the ceiling, only centimeters from their lips, were thousands and thousands of hairy spiders.

He didn't want to look too closely at them, but he was forced to because he was nose-to-nose with them.

They were so close to them that he could count the hairs on their legs and see the light beams glisten off their teeth. Each furry black spider had to be the size of his fist.

Audrey tried to scream, but in doing so, she had lost her focus on treading water, and her momentary lapse in judgment sent her head below the water.

As she came up for air again, Jonah placed his free hand over her mouth to silence her.

"If you scream again, you may startle the spiders into action. I don't know if these things are venomous, but I'm not trying to find out. They're probably just trying to escape the rising waters, just like we are."

He shined his light toward the ceiling behind him, where he

could see some of the spiders begin to get pulled from the rock by the rising water. Looking around, he could see that many of the spiders had fallen victim to the water, and they were currently floating around them.

In the face of trying to keep Audrey from having another panic attack, he wasn't going to bring up the floating spiders. Instead, he caught some movement out of the corner of his eye.

Shining his light toward the spiders on the ceiling, many of them seemed to be moving in one direction.

Then he remembered what he had thought of earlier.

"If the water is still coming in, that means that the air has someplace to go, which means that there is another exit in here somewhere," Jonah said excitedly to Audrey. "And I bet you those spiders are headed that way to escape the water!"

Following the direction of the spiders, Jonah paddled over to the other side of the cave. Shining his light back at the ceiling again, he saw it.

Previously hidden by a large outcrop of rock, he could see a rusty iron ladder. The ladder led upwards to another area currently hidden by the rock.

They needed to get up there, but their time was running out.

Jonah shined his light back toward Audrey, but she was nowhere to be found.

The ceiling was lower on the other side of the cave, and she had just taken her last breath. That side of the cave was completely underwater.

"Audrey!" Jonah called out. After hearing no response, he took a deep breath, preparing himself to go in after her.

Then he felt an arm tug him underwater.

He flailed around, kicking and screaming until his flashlight caught on something bright. It was Audrey's face.

They both resurfaced, gasping for air.

"You have to stop doing that," Jonah exclaimed.

"Sorry," Audrey replied between gasps of air. "I was busy drowning."

Jonah pointed his light at the ladder above them. "I found the way out."

Chapter Fifty-Five

"Ew, ew, ew, ew!" Audrey squealed.

They had just climbed to the top of the iron ladder, which led them to what appeared to be a tunnel system that led throughout the island.

Once Jonah had switched his light back on, however, Audrey had gotten a glimpse of the thousands of spiders that had recently taken refuge here to escape the rising flood.

The walls were so thick with them that it resembled a dirty shag carpet. And they didn't stick to covering the walls alone.

A quick swipe of the flashlight across the floor revealed what appeared to be waves of movement as the spiders migrated to a new location.

"We have to find out where this tunnel leads," Jonah said. He held out his hand toward Audrey, who hesitated. "Our only other option is to stay here and wait for the spiders to cover us like they're covering these walls."

That seemed to do the trick.

Audrey quickly grabbed Jonah's hand and began following him through the halls.

Devin Cabrera

They walked slowly through the tunnel, not knowing what was awaiting them around each bend. They tried to walk as quietly as they could, but it was almost impossible. The carpet of spiders beneath their feet was hard not to step on, and each step they took made a resounding crunch as a spider's life was pulverized beneath their soles.

Though Audrey didn't mind ending the life of a giant spider, she did not envy the cleanup she would have to look forward to when this was all over. She could only imagine picking hundreds of legs out of the tracks of her sneakers. At this point, she would prefer just to throw them out and walk home barefoot. If they ever got the chance to leave this place, that is.

They rounded a bend in the tunnel. The bulk of the spiders hadn't made it this far, and in their absence, they were able to make out more of their surroundings.

The walls around them seemed to be carved out of limestone, with beams every five feet or so to support the weight of the earth on top of them, keeping the tunnel from collapsing altogether.

The spiders disappeared into giant cracks in the walls and ceiling of the tunnel, where ice must have formed over the years, expanding in the cracks, and creating a path from the topside down. Being that it was raining above ground, the saturated earth seemed to be giving way, creating thousands of water droplets along the ceiling which constantly rained down upon them.

The sound in the tunnel was a conundrum of dripping water, spider legs moving, and the sound of their footsteps against the stone ground. It was so loud that Jonah couldn't hear himself think. So, it was a total surprise to him when they rounded a corner of the tunnel and came face to face with a door.

Jonah looked at Audrey, pointing toward the door. It took a while to gain her attention, as her eyes were fixated on the spiders around them.

Audrey's eyes lit up when she saw the door. She reached for the handle, glad to be anywhere other than in a tunnel filled with spiders.

Welcome To Nightmare Island

Jonah held up a hand as if to tell Audrey to wait.

They didn't know what was behind this door. Knowing this island, it could be any manner of cruel things. They hadn't walked through a single door on this trip that didn't lead them to something much worse on the other side.

Miles and his goons could be on the other side of the door. Miles had tricked them into coming to this island and had left them stranded in a storm with no protection from its homicidal tenants. Who knows what he would do to them if he found them down here.

Would Miles kill them himself? Send his goons to do it for him? To finish off the job that he had set in motion above ground?

What if it wasn't Miles? At least if it was him, then they could fight someone human. It could be a ghost, one so bad that they wouldn't even feature it on the tour. Kept down here for safekeeping, unreachable by humans. If it were a ghost, they wouldn't have a chance at getting away. They couldn't kill a ghost, and they couldn't run either. The way that they had come was now blocked by water and a wall of spiders.

No. Their only option was forward.

Jonah slowly bent his head down, placing his ear against the cold metal of the door. He listened for as long as he could before picking his head back up.

He couldn't hear a thing on the other side. This may be because there was nothing there. Or it could mean that the door was just so thick that it had become soundproof. It didn't help that Jonah couldn't hear anything over the sounds of the bugs and water cascading in around them.

There was nothing else left to do. He had to go for it.

Jonah reached for the brass handle. It was cold in his hand and covered with a light mist from the condensation in the air.

He turned the handle and pushed, and to his surprise, the door opened smoothly.

Jonah held his breath as the door swung open, waiting to see what terrifying thing awaited them on the other side.

Devin Cabrera

What they saw was more shocking than anything they could have imagined.

Chapter Fifty-Six

The door swung open to reveal Maverick Knight.
It was the man that they had saved from the hotel. They had last seen him when they had made a break for it across the island. Jonah had tripped, and due to it being so dark, his friends had all crashed into him and fallen over as well. Maverick had been in the front of the group and had not realized that they had stopped. He had continued to his destination without them, leaving them defenseless against the ghosts on the island.

Maverick was disheveled and had a long gash on his face. His hair was matted to his head on one side where he must have been injured, the blood of an open wound turning his hair into a solid chunk.

Jonah walked inside the room toward Maverick. He was about to greet him like a friend who had the ability to get them off the island, when he caught something out of the corner of his eye.

One wall of the room was completely covered by television monitors. On the screens were images that Jonah and Audrey knew all too well.

Just then, Audrey walked into the room, mouth agape at the display before her.

The screens before them showed all the different parts of the island.

Every house. Every building. Each location that they had been to tonight was mapped out in front of them in vivid detail.

Jonah didn't know what to say. He felt a sudden rage building up in him that he couldn't contain.

Suddenly, he turned on Maverick.

"The whole time?" Jonah screamed at Maverick. "The whole time that we were out there fighting for our lives, you were down here watching us like it was some kind of sporting event?"

"No, no. It's not like that!" Maverick said, putting his hands up in front of him.

"You've been down here with cameras watching our every move. You saw us walking into rooms with ghosts. You could have warned us. You could have gotten us and brought us to safety. But instead, you watched as our friends were killed in front of us. And you did nothing!" Jonah's head was throbbing. The amount of rage that was building up inside him made him feel like he was on the verge of hurting someone. He might just kill Maverick for the fun of it.

"No! Please, let me explain!" Maverick said in response. "We were all on our way here after you found me. After we ran off into the storm, we lost track of each other. I turned around at one point and none of you were there. I turned back, running into the storm looking for you all but I couldn't find any of you. Instead, I ended up running into Jones Jepsen."

Maverick pointed at his head, where the blood had pooled and clotted in his hair. "I had to try to fight him off. He got in a few good shots before I was able to escape through a secret passage and come down here. Once I got here, I ran into one of Miles's goons." With this, Maverick pointed at a man's body in the corner of the room that they had not yet noticed.

Jonah recognized the man. He was the one they had met at the beginning of the tour. This was the man who had portrayed Maverick when they first got on the island.

Welcome To Nightmare Island

Maverick continued. "Though Miles had already stolen the orb that powers the barriers on the island, I had installed a secondary device down here that would power up the bracelets on your wrists." With this, he raised his hand, showing the useless piece of metal on his wrist that no longer glowed blue.

"The system down here runs on the same generator that powers the cameras. It's separate from the main generator outside. A backup if you will. The only problem is that if the orb is removed from its place, the bracelet system must be restarted by hand. When I got down here, Miles's goon had been watching the cameras. He knew that I was coming, and he took a knife to the bracelet system, making it unusable."

Maverick pointed to a system against one of the walls that looked kind of like a bank atm. Now, the screen was flashing random colors and shooting out sparks from several holes in it.

"Once I entered the room, he turned the knife on me."

Jonah looked at the gash on Maverick's face. It hadn't had time to heal yet, and the blood was still dripping down his face at an alarming rate.

"I was able to subdue the guard down here in the control room. However, as for your friends, there was nothing I could do. I'm sorry," Maverick said, dropping his head down low.

"But you're supposed to be the best ghost hunter in the world," Audrey said. "Why don't you go out there and handle the ghosts?"

"It's not that easy," Maverick said. "Without the orb, I have no power over the ghosts. The only reason I had become the world's best ghost hunter is because I created the orb. I was the only one with the technology that could handle such things. Before that, ancient civilizations would ignore the problem or treat ghosts as gods. They would offer up their people as sacrifices to spare their own lives. Before I had the orb, I had no power over the ghosts. I had as much power as a priest. I would go from door to door performing exorcisms and hoping the problem would go away on its own, like a placebo. Without the orb, there's nothing any of us can do to stop the ghosts on this island. Me intervening when your friends were attacked would only succeed in giving the ghosts another body to feed on."

Jonah's head dropped as he plopped down in the chair in front of the wall of screens. He knew he wasn't mad at Maverick, he just wanted someone to blame.

"The only thing we can do is get off this island and get far away. Once we're away from here, I can try to get the orb back from Miles or find some way to create a new one. One thing is for sure, nobody is safe here," Maverick said.

Jonah and Audrey stared up at the screens. The ghosts had given up looking for them at the edge of the cliff and had begun roaming the island once more, looking for other bodies to feed on.

Jones Jepsen had found Henry's body near the signal tower and had decided to play with it. He had picked him up and begun to waltz around the grounds with Henry's corpse.

This made Jonah scowl. He had liked Henry. The man had the kind of southern twang that made him sound like he didn't know much, but he knew everything that he needed to get by. It was comforting to hear, especially when many of the other voices on the island belonged to those who wanted them dead.

In the top right corner, Jonah saw movement.

It was the dock that they had come in on. The friends had been running around for so long that the sun had begun to rise. With it came the one thing they were waiting for since they walked onto this godforsaken island.

It was the boat.

Chapter Fifty-Seven

Jonah pointed it out to Audrey and Maverick, who rushed over to see. It was indeed the boat off the island. The man in the cloak was rowing toward the dock, eager to get his cargo and get out of there.

As they watched, the man pulled the boat up to the dock and tied it off. Then he looked around, presumably looking for his passengers.

They were presently otherwise occupied.

The man seemed to be getting impatient, pulling up his sleeve to look at his watch.

"We have to get to the dock!" Jonah shouted. He turned to Maverick. "What is the fastest way to the dock?"

Maverick seemed like he was about to answer when they heard a noise coming from the screen that showed the dock. They swung their heads around to see what it was.

The man on the boat seemed to hear it too. His head snapped toward the direction of the island. He had just heard dogs barking. The sound of the vicious growling and snapping of the Huntsman and his hounds.

And they were getting closer.

The three people in the control room watched one of the other monitors as the hounds traveled from screen to screen, getting closer and closer to the dock. They had smelled fresh blood, and the Huntsman had sent them out for their next kill.

Miles had told them that the locals were very superstitious, and the man on the boat was no exception. He had heard stories of what was on this island, though he had never seen anything with his own eyes before. He wasn't going to stick around and find out what it was.

As Jonah and his friends looked on in horror, the man untied his boat from the dock and began to row off into the fog.

The hounds ran right to the edge of the dock, their paws clinging to the wood surface, keeping them from falling into the water. There they stood, howling at the boat as they watched their next meal slip away from them.

Jonah was distraught. He slipped out of the chair onto the floor, where he lay cradling his knees. Tonight, he had watched all his friends die in front of him. Audrey was the only one he had left. His one solace was that eventually, the boat would come, and they would have an opportunity to leave this place. Now that boat was gone, and so was their chance of getting off this island. This meant that their one chance of surviving was over. The ghosts would come for them, and he would eventually have to watch Audrey get murdered in front of him. He didn't know if he could take that kind of heartache. He didn't know how much more of anything that he could take. He was slowly losing his mind as everything that he did began to turn on him.

Audrey bent down to comfort Jonah, but it was no use. There was nothing that she could say that could make him feel better because she didn't have any options either. She was one thing going wrong away from joining him on the floor.

That's when Maverick piped up from the other side of the room.

"All hope may not be lost just yet. There is another boat off the island," Maverick said.

This piqued Jonah's attention. He looked up from his spot on the floor. "Where is it?" Jonah asked.

Welcome To Nightmare Island

"It's near one of the back corners of the island. We have a boathouse on site for instances just like this. I was concerned that one day the superstitions of the locals would grow too much, and they might never come back with the boat, so one day I brought my own. And it's a good thing I did too, considering what happened just now. That guy is never coming back."

Jonah stood up, walking over to where Maverick stood. "Take us to that boat."

Maverick moved over to the wall of screens. He filtered through a few of the cameras until he found the one, he wanted. This one appeared to show the outside of a boathouse, and just outside of the front of it, they could see the tip of a boat bobbing in the water.

"Good. It's still there," Maverick said in a relieved tone. "I wasn't sure if Miles had taken it or if he had brought his own boat to the island to leave on. The fact that this boat is still there means that Miles left on his own boat. Or he's still on the island somewhere. Either way, we have to hurry."

Chapter Fifty-Eight

Maverick grabbed a flashlight off the wall and ushered Jonah and Audrey back into the tunnel.

"During wartime, the owners of the asylum had a bunker commissioned down here for the staff to escape to in case planes were heard overhead," Maverick said as they walked. "They created tunnels underground that lead to just about everywhere on the island. Wherever the staff were, they would be able to get to their nearest passage opening and get to safety, rather than running to a central location where they might be spotted from the air."

He stopped for a moment, swinging his flashlight this way and that, as if he were trying to remember his way around.

"This way."

They followed Maverick through a tunnel that looked like it had never been used after it had been created. At certain points the roof sloped forward, making it so that they needed to crouch to continue walking. This part of the tunnel clearly hadn't been serviced in a long time. The beams that held up the ceiling were wet and rotted in several places, with chunks of wood having fallen off completely. Stalactites hung from the ceiling, creating another obstacle that the group had to dodge as they walked to prevent them from impaling themselves. As they grew closer to their destination, Jonah recognized a familiar odor.

It was a combination of the smell of death and the odor of moist earth. It was the smell of a fresh grave.

Jonah looked up, and to his horror, he saw bone fragments sticking out of the ceiling of the tunnel where some of the rock had collapsed.

Maverick turned back to check on them, to make sure he hadn't lost them again. That's when he saw Jonah's horrified expression. He followed Jonah's eye line and instantly realized what had happened.

"The boathouse which we are going to is on the other side of the island. To get to it, we must pass underneath the cemetery. The tunnel was built before many of the graves had been dug, and over time the earth has begun to wash away, revealing the bones of those who have died here. Occasionally I have heard the moans of the dead in these halls. I would suspect that their spirits had gotten in through here," Maverick said pointing toward the bones threatening to reach down and grab them.

"Unfortunately for us, you're not going to like where this tunnel leads," Maverick said as he continued through the passage.

They would soon find out why.

The air began to grow stuffier as they walked. The smell of death began to become overpowering as the bones were replaced by tree roots snaking down from the ceiling and threatening to strangle them upon one misstep.

Finally, they came to the end of the tunnel.

It was a dead end. Or at least, that's what it looked like.

They had been expecting a doorway or a trapdoor leading to a building above ground. What they got instead was a wall covered in plant growth. Roots the color of bone stretched from the ceiling down to the floor, creating a mass so thick that they couldn't see through it.

Maverick had to improvise. After he had been kidnapped by Miles's goons, he hadn't been left with a knife or any other weapons.

He looked around the passage, searching for something that he could use to cut through the wall of roots. He bent down to pick up a rock that had fallen from the walls. One end had been sheared off, creating a sharp edge. He took the rock back over to the wall and using both hands he swung it at the roots.

It was slow work until Jonah found a similar rock and began to help. Together they were able to create a sizeable hole in the wall of roots. Behind it was something that Jonah and Audrey weren't expecting.

It was a casket.

"Help me out with this," Maverick said to Jonah.

Under Maverick's direction, Jonah took up a place on one side of the casket. They placed their hands on the cold stone box and pushed. It was heavy. Partially because it was made from stone and partially because the thing hadn't been moved in hundreds of years. Jonah felt like the thing had become part of the earth as the ground has slowly begun to reclaim it.

They gave another push, and the casket began to move. The box made a grinding noise as the stone-on-stone surfaces met.

Finally, with one last push, the casket fell off its perch and crashed to the ground on the other side.

There was another room on the other side.

Jonah tried to look through the hole where the casket once stood, but the room on the other side was pitch black.

"There's our way out," Maverick said pointing toward the hole. "After you."

Jonah handed his flashlight to Audrey, then began to climb through the hole. It was a tight squeeze, and it reminded him of when he climbed through the air vents in the library. He shook his head, trying to rid himself of that image. Now was not the time to dredge up thoughts about his friends who had died that night. He made it to the other side, then helped Audrey and Maverick through the hole.

The room that they were in was damp and deathly quiet, though something about it seemed very familiar to Jonah. In a moment he would find out why.

Audrey handed Jonah's flashlight back to him after climbing through the hole in the wall. He flipped it on and swung it around him to get a picture of his surroundings.

Now he knew why the room felt familiar.

They were in the crypt of the Black Witch.

Chapter Fifty-Nine

Jonah stopped where he was. There was something off about the room that he couldn't put his finger on.

Maverick noticed it too.

The room was quiet.

Normally the screams of the Black Witch could be heard from above ground but right now they couldn't hear anything at all. They should hear her screaming and protesting, trying to get out of the tomb that she had been chained inside.

Maverick shone his flashlight up at the stone coffin in the center of the room. To his horror, the chains had been broken off. The lid itself, which had to weigh a ton, had been launched off the coffin and thrown across the room, where it now lay shattered in pieces on the ground.

Jonah and Audrey stood their ground, while Maverick slowly inched his way toward the stone coffin. He walked up the steps made of bones, making a loud crack echo around the room as a skull splintered beneath his feet.

But Maverick took no notice of the noise. His mind was too

focused on what was in the coffin, or for that matter, what wasn't inside it.

The coffin was empty.

The Black Witch was gone.

Maverick took only a moment to think before running back to Audrey and Jonah.

"We have to get out of here now!" Maverick said, pulling them along with him as he made his way toward the stairs leading above ground. "If the witch is out, that means that nobody is safe anymore. This island has become ground zero."

Jonah and Audrey followed Maverick as he led the way up the stairs.

"Wasn't there a switch that was supposed to keep the Witch from escaping the crypt?" Audrey asked.

Maverick stopped on the stairs to examine a box that was hardwired into the wall. As he followed the wire, he came to a stop.

The wire had been chewed through by rats.

"Normally this sensor was supposed to acknowledge whenever a paranormal entity was present on the stairwell, and it would automatically trigger an explosion which would bring the earth down on top of her tomb. Rats must have chewed through the wires, leaving the sensor useless. It was Henry's job to go around and make sure that these types of things were up to par. He had gotten busy on some other projects on the island and thought that this one could wait as the orb was keeping the Witch in place. He couldn't have known that something like this would happen," Maverick said, dropping his head. He clearly had a soft spot for the old man from Louisiana.

They continued up the stairs to the heavy iron door. There they halted, Maverick putting his finger up to his lips to indicate that they should keep quiet. He peeked over the window, looking to see if there were any ghosts outside, but he couldn't see a thing.

Maverick reached for the handle, slowly opening the crypt door. He cringed as the ancient door hinges squealed in protest. He knew he should've pushed Henry to focus more energy on the Black Witch's crypt. But the man didn't like coming down to this part of the island and Maverick couldn't blame him. He had spent the bulk of his life being a ghosthunter and whenever he heard the Black Witch's screams it put him on edge and made the hairs on the back of his neck rise.

He let go of the door handle, waiting to see if anything popped out of the shadows. A dense fog had rolled in, covering up the sunrise once more. They waited in silence, but nothing came for them. It was eerily quiet here.

Maverick stepped outside, making a motion for Jonah and Audrey to do the same.

They hesitated with each step they took, not wanting to direct any unwanted attention toward themselves. But just like Maverick, they found nothing waiting for them outside of the crypt.

"Which way is the boathouse?" Jonah asked quietly.

"It's this way," Maverick said pointing into the fog. He led them into the cemetery, being careful not to trip over any of the headstones and unkempt tree roots.

Jonah looked back at the crypt they had recently left, but the fog had already swallowed it whole.

They kept on like this for a while, until suddenly the fog shifted before them. It was like a cold breeze had swept in, sending a chill through all their spines.

It also cleared a giant section of the fog around them. Ahead, they could see the outline of the boathouse in the distance.

Audrey's confidence rose when she saw the boathouse. She gained a bit of energy that she didn't know still existed in her after what she had been through tonight. She started to run for the boathouse, but Jonah reached his arm out to stop her.

She turned to face him and realized that he and Maverick were staring off into the distance at something. While she had focused on the boathouse, she had missed something important that had appeared in front of them.

As the fog cleared around them, it revealed a ghost standing over a tombstone. As she looked around, Audrey could see that it wasn't the only one. There were hundreds of them hovering nearby.

They were surrounded.

"These are the ghosts of the dead that have been buried on the island," Maverick said. "Without the orb suppressing the amount of supernatural activity on the island, those who had died here are now able to walk free once more. They're harmless. These types of ghosts generally haunt small homes and will terrify the owners. Powerful enough to haunt but not to harm. Before I created the orb, these kinds of ghosts were my bread and butter. It's the big ghosts that we must worry about. The kind that I had locked up on this island."

Jonah looked around at the ghosts who surrounded them. He recognized some of their outfits. He saw plenty of nurses dressed in scrubs, as well as those dressed in gowns who Jonah gathered were the patients of the asylum that had died here. As he spun around, a certain group of ghosts caught his eye.

He recognized them.

Jonah had seen a painting of them above the mantle at Graystone Manor.

He was looking at the ghosts of the Graystone family.

Mr. Graystone stood near his kids. They looked just like they did in the painting, except for one thing. In death, they still showed the wounds that killed them.

Mr. Graystone was missing half of his face. His children, who clung to their father's side, had distinguishable lines across their throats.

Mrs. Graystone, however, stood farther back from the rest of the family. She had been buried near the rest of the family but in a separate plot due to the circumstance of their deaths. Her throat had several long gashes across it, exposing the raw muscle underneath. A razor blade still stuck out of the side of her neck. Her eyes were solid white as if someone had stolen her pupils. But even without pupils, Jonah could tell that she was staring daggers at the backs of her families' heads. There was an anger there that hadn't died with her death.

Jonah forced himself to look away. Seeing the family had filled him with the utmost despair, and he had to think of happy thoughts to get himself to look away.

In doing so, Jonah noticed the expressions on the rest of the ghost's faces. He was confused. He had spent so much time focused on the Graystone family ghosts that he hadn't noticed what was going on with the other ghosts around them.

They were dead, but even in death, they seemed fearful. Of what, Jonah wasn't sure just yet.

The ghosts weren't looking at Jonah and the others. They were looking past them.

What could scare something that was already dead?

Chapter Sixty

Just then, they heard a loud croaking noise from behind them.
They whipped around, just in time to see a ghost crawl out from behind the veil of fog.
Crawling was a nice way to put it, however, it wasn't the most accurate description of how she moved.

As she moved toward them, her bones seemed to snap at inhuman angles. They cracked and splintered as she walked, moving like a contortionist whose body bent in places that shouldn't be possible.

"It's the Black Witch," Maverick said with a notable amount of fear in his voice. He took a few steps backward, whispering to Jonah and Audrey, "She lived an extraordinarily evil life. So much so that when she was finally killed, the devil himself sentenced her spirit to walk the earth in constant unbearable pain."

At the sound of his voice, the Black Witch stopped moving. Her body stood still, but her head twisted around like an owl to face him. In doing so, they heard her neck bones breaking several times over.

Her face was the most horrible thing they could imagine. Greasy black hair came down across her face, almost hiding the dark pits where her eyes should have been. Based on the scars that covered her face, it was reasonable to believe that her eyes had been clawed out. Of the teeth that she had, several were black and rotten. The skin and muscle on one side of her upper lip had been torn off, revealing her skull from her upper jaw to where her nose should have been. In the place of her nose, there were just two holes where the cartilage once was.

"Did the devil do that to her too?" Jonah asked Maverick in a whisper.

"No. Back when she was alive, she had killed many people who came near her cabin. Eventually, she was hunted down by villagers who had gotten up the nerve to face her. They mortally wounded her, and then set her cabin on fire with her inside. Unfortunately for the Black Witch, she lived through the fire but was injured too much to move. Afterward, the buzzards had come down upon her cabin, having smelled the charred remains of her body. They pecked out her eyes and tore off chunks of her face while she lay there, unable to do anything about it. Eventually, she succumbed to her injuries and died. That's when the devil decided she hadn't been punished enough and sent her back for more."

The Black Witch was on all fours now. Her head twisted from side to side. Just then she let out a piercing scream, leaving them all to press their hands to their ears to keep from going deaf. Then the Witch crawled slowly forward, letting out a long croak. She tilted her head again as if she was listening.

Jonah realized that because she had no eyes, she was using a form of echolocation, creating sound, and then listening for the reverb to be able to tell what she was around.

"When I tell you to run, you run," Maverick whispered to Jonah and Audrey.

The Black Witch stopped in her tracks. Her lack of sight had created an opportunity for her hearing to become advanced beyond measure. She had heard Maverick's voice.

And she recognized him.

Welcome To Nightmare Island

This was the man who had captured her and put her in a box. For years she had screamed endlessly, trying to get out, unable to do anything but press against the underside of the caskets stone lid.

It had been years since she had heard his voice, but it was the last thing she heard before being put in the box. This gave her ample time to replay that voice repeatedly in her head. And she was ready for revenge.

Maverick slowly stepped to his left, putting some distance between himself and where Jonah and Audrey stood. He stepped on a twig, its snap causing the Black Witch's head to tilt in his direction.

"RUN!" Maverick screamed at Jonah and Audrey.

At that moment, the Black Witch launched herself toward Maverick. Her fingers clawed at the ground as she moved, ripping the earth apart as she made her deadly ascent toward the man who had imprisoned her for years.

At the same time, Jonah grabbed Audrey's hand and pulled her toward the boathouse. Audrey looked back over her shoulder at Maverick, but there was nothing that they could do for him now.

Maverick moved to get out of the way, but there was nothing that he could do to stop the Black Witch. Without the orb, there was nothing stopping her from attacking him.

She leaped from a crouched position, hitting Maverick's body, and bringing him down to the ground.

Jonah didn't bother turning around. He didn't want to put an image to the awful sounds that he was hearing. It was the sounds of bones breaking, of arms being ripped out of their sockets. They could hear Maverick's screams of pain all the way down to the boathouse.

Suddenly, with a snap, Maverick's screams ended.

Chapter Sixty-One

Jonah and Audrey opened the door to the boathouse. To their relief, there appeared to be a fully functioning boat inside.

What they were not expecting, however, was that the boathouse wouldn't be empty.

Standing next to the boat was Miles.

Their attention was distracted from Miles by a pulsing blue light coming from inside the boat.

With a shock, they realized that it was the orb. The one thing that had the power to keep them safe from the ghosts outside this room was sitting inside that boat.

Jonah and Audrey stood still, waiting for Miles to notice their arrival. They fully expected him to turn around and try to hurt them, to keep them on this island until the ghosts could finish them off for him.

But as they waited, Miles never moved.

Without taking his eyes off Miles, Jonah slowly inched his way around him until he could see his face.

Miles's eyes were rolled back inside his head. He seemed lost in a trance, still bent over to load what he needed into the boat. But his

Welcome To Nightmare Island

face was turned in a direction that made it seem like he had heard something in the boathouse. Something that had surprised him.

Jonah followed Miles's line of sight, only to scramble backward.

They weren't alone in the boathouse.

Mabel was standing on the other side of the room. Her eyes were locked onto Miles's own.

She must have come upon Miles while he was trying to escape, Jonah thought. Once he had been surprised by the ghost, she must have put him in a trance, one which would give them enough time to get in the boat and leave this foul place once and for all.

Jonah said a silent thank you in Mabel's direction.

He indicated for Audrey to follow him, and quietly they loaded into the boat. Jonah reached for the orb. The box that contained it must have fallen when Miles had been entranced by Mable. It now lay on its side, slightly cracked open, revealing the pulsing blue contents inside.

Jonah grabbed the box and closed it. This may be the key to preventing ghosts from taking over his world, he wasn't going to let it flop around the boat like a dying fish.

Audrey stared out into the opening of the boathouse. As she watched, the never-ending fog seemed to lift, revealing the sun. She had to shield her eyes with her hand. It was so warm and bright; unlike anything they had experienced for the last few days.

Mabel noticed it too, and she didn't seem pleased.

As the sunlight filled the boathouse, Mabel shrunk away from it, disappearing into the darkness.

It was like a switch had been flipped.

Miles woke up from his trance in an instant. He was in a manic state, looking around for the ghosts which were no doubt about to end his life. His eyes were wide as he came back from the nightmare that Mabel had just put him through.

As he wheeled around, he didn't see any ghosts.

Instead, he found Jonah and Audrey about to take off in the boat with the orb that he had worked so hard to get.

Miles knew he couldn't get left behind on this island with all the ghosts who probably wanted more than anything to kill him. He had to act immediately.

Miles sprung to his feet, and in a flash, he grabbed Jonah and pulled him out of the boat and onto the dock that stood next to it. If he could take out Jonah, then Audrey probably wouldn't be much of an issue to handle. And he knew that she wouldn't leave Jonah behind.

Jonah struggled from beneath Miles's grasp. He hadn't expected the man to move so fast. One moment he was on the boat and the next moment Miles was on top of him, with his hands around Jonah's throat.

Jonah kicked up at Miles, but his attempts were feeble. He had exhausted so much of his energy just getting to where he was tonight, that he didn't have much left to fight Miles off with. Jonah tried to pull Miles's fingers off his throat, but the man's grasp only seemed to get tighter.

Jonah had to switch up tactics. If he was going to get out of this, he was going to have to get on the offensive. He moved his hands up toward Miles's face, digging his thumbs into the man's eye sockets.

Miles screamed, but he kept going. He knew that if he was going to succeed at this, he was going to have to push through whatever Jonah sent his way. It was either this or deal with the ghosts on the island, and that would only end up worse for him.

Jonah pressed as hard as he could into Miles's eye sockets, but he could feel his energy draining. His vision was becoming blurry as he struggled to retain enough oxygen. His hands fell away, and just as he felt the world going black, he heard a noise.

CLANG!

Audrey had come up from behind Miles and hit him on the head with her long metal flashlight.

Miles fell to the ground with a thud. Audrey had knocked him out with one swing.

Jonah got up on all fours, struggling to make up for all the breath that he had lost. He knew he didn't have much time, so he pulled himself onto the boat, letting his body hit the bottom as he did so.

Audrey grabbed the rope that moored the boat to the boathouse dock, and she flung it away. Then she reached for the oars and began to push off, sending the boat floating off into the lake.

Jonah sat up, taking one of the oars from Audrey.

Together, they rowed into the sunrise.

When they were a few hundred feet away from the shore, Miles groggily sat up. He reached a hand up to where Audrey had hit him with the flashlight but winced when he touched the spot. Suddenly, he came to his senses, remembering what had happened. Miles spun around, searching for the orb.

But the orb and the boat were missing.

Miles looked out toward the lake and saw Jonah and Audrey floating away. His only ride off the island was leaving, along with the thing he had come here to get.

"Come back here!" Miles screamed.

But Jonah and Audrey kept going.

Miles ran into the murky waters before him but stopped once he got to the point where his feet no longer touched the ground beneath him. Miles didn't know how to swim. Cursing to himself, he made the trek back to shore.

There, Miles collapsed onto the ground, defeated.

Jonah and Audrey continued to row toward home.

As they did so, a thick fog began to return to the island, slowly swallowing all its buildings whole.

In the distance, they began to hear the hounds howling. Followed by the maniacal cackling of a homicidal maniac.

Epilogue

Jonah sat at a table during a book signing at a bookstore in Portsmouth, New Hampshire.

A young teenager came up to his table, sliding a copy of Jonah's latest book across to him.

"Can you make it out to Jacob?" the teen asked.

"Sure thing, kid."

Jonah grabbed the copy of Nightmare Island and opened the cover. Inside, on the dedications page, he had printed a very special dedication.

"This book is dedicated to Chuck, Annie, Kevin, and Maverick. May their spirits rest in peace."

Jonah signed the book for the kid, then took what was probably the hundredth selfie with a fan that day.

He called for the next person in line to come up, tapping his pen anxiously. This was a tic that he sometimes did when he felt like he was standing in one space too long. Though he loved his fans and loved even better that his books had become a huge success, Jonah would much rather be at home right now, possibly penning out another best seller.

Welcome To Nightmare Island

Jonah was too lost in thought to notice the next person in line until the man had blocked out the light with his body. This guy was much bigger than Jonah's normal fanbase.

Jonah looked up to see a huge man in a trench coat and sunglasses. His hat was pulled down low, hiding his face in darkness.

"Who should I make this one out to?" Jonah asked.

As the man slid the book across the table, Jonah noticed something odd on the man's wrist. It was a tattoo of a ram skull over a pentagram.

The same insignia which was carved into the lid of Jonah's pocket watch.

About the Author

Devin Cabrera developed a passion for stories at a young age, devouring books at every turn. As an adult, this love of stories turned into a career, working on both the big and small screen, bringing characters to life and captivating audiences. With a diverse range of projects under his belt, from gripping dramas such as Pretty Little Liars to thrilling reality shows like Deadliest Catch, he has proven himself as an excellent storyteller in all its forms.

But it wasn't until recently that he decided to turn his talents to the page. Sitting down at his desk, he painstakingly crafted a story, honing every word until it was just right. With a fresh perspective and a lifetime of experience with stories, he promises to take readers on a journey they won't soon forget.

Also by Devin Cabrera

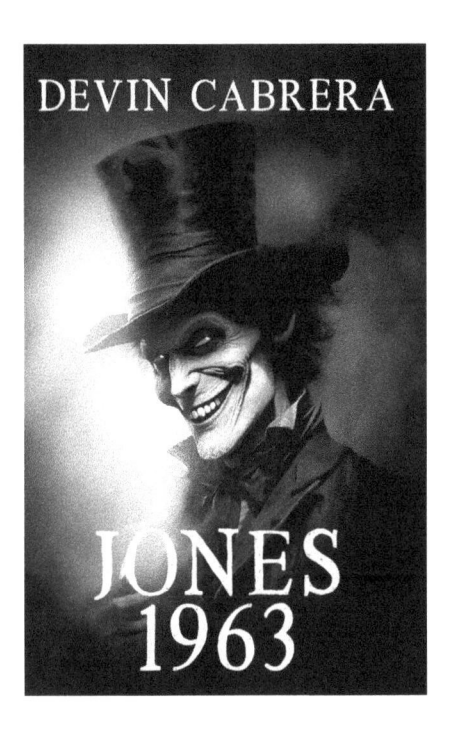

In the once-tranquil town of Briarwood, 1963 marked the year when peace shattered into chaos. A lifetime of torment and humiliation pushed Jones Jepsen to the brink, and within him, a dormant darkness awakened.

In a chilling rampage driven by a thirst for revenge, Jones embarks on a spree of violence that shakes the very foundation of Briarwood. As the body count rises, the town's inhabitants find themselves trapped in a nightmare, asking the harrowing question: Will anyone be safe from the wrath of Jones? In this heart-pounding tale of vengeance and suspense, the battle for survival takes center stage, and the fate of Briarwood hangs in the balance.

www.ingramcontent.com/pod-product-compliance
Ingram Content Group UK Ltd.
Pitfield, Milton Keynes, MK11 3LW, UK
UKHW031614020125
3924UKWH00025B/244